THE ILLEST

© 2014, 2019 Randolph Walker, Jr.
Cover image used courtesy of Judeus Samson

10 9 8 7 6 5 4 3 2

ISBN: 9781020001086

45 Alternate Press, LLC
Hampton, Virginia

THE ILLEST

A NOVELLA

RAN WALKER

CONTENTS

1

BROOKLYN

Even after a week, Troy Dobbs still had yet to completely adjust to Aunt Flo's brownstone. It was far more spacious than the dorm room he had occupied over the past four years, and it was also much nicer than anything he had lived in, including his parents' house just off the bay in Gloucester, Virginia.

The decorations throughout the brownstone reflected an entirely different level of cultural sophistication than he was accustomed to. There were carved masks from Nairobi, signed prints by various African-American artists, and black & white photographs that were matted and framed featuring Aunt Flo alongside celebrities, politicians, and potentates. The furniture was sparse, yet fly, and ceiling-high bookcases stretched along two entire walls of the living room, packed with books from a myriad of African-American, Caribbean, and African writers. There was even a piece of a wood (part of a door maybe?) with Jean-Michel

Basquiat's discernible handwriting, accompanied by his trademark crown. Against the rest of the artifacts of Aunt Flo's Cabinet of Curiosities, Troy didn't need to question its authenticity. He was, after all, in Brooklyn, and such things, as he was learning, were not completely unheard of.

The Notorious B.I.G. had passed away only three months earlier, and Brooklyn was wrestling with one of its most significant losses in years, yet it was still poised on the verge of declaring itself the new, undisputed capital of Planet Hip-Hop. Of course, Biggie's home neighborhood of Bed Stuy was a far cry from the Huxtable-like comfort of Aunt Flo's Brooklyn Heights neighborhood, but to Troy it was still *technically* Brooklyn and therefore good enough to embrace and throw his hands in the air whenever he heard Biggie rap the famous phrase, "Is Brooklyn in the house?"

Aunt Flo was out globetrotting with her latest male companion (a French model fifteen years her junior, Troy had heard), this time on a European cruise that departed from Barcelona. Her graduation gift to her only nephew was to leave the keys to her brownstone, a building of which she occupied all three floors (and basement) by herself, and have him housesit for the month that she would be away. And even though he had not yet gotten used to the amazing view of the skyline of Manhattan from the promenade view outside the kitchen window, he was gradually acclimating himself to the neighborhood, having found a breakfast diner on the corner of Henry and Clark and several great lunch and dinner spots along Montague Street.

His bedroom was on the second floor of the house, just

off from the den area and down the hall from the kitchen. This was also the floor that housed the master bedroom and, from the clear look of things, the floor Aunt Flo occupied most. Artwork filled the halls, and personal photographs in small frames rested on the edges of freshly polished shelves.

Troy was not completely sure he knew what Aunt Flo did for a living, but he knew she had been married to a media mogul for ten years and had come away from that situation pretty well off. Since then she had become a bon vivant in a family full of people who neither had the time nor the interest in hedonistic socializing.

While Troy had been to Aunt Flo's home once several years back, he never imagined he would have the full run of the place. Each morning he awoke pinching himself and reminding himself of his amazing fortune. This awestruck state occupied most of his first week, and by the time he made it to Sunday morning, he had collapsed on the chaise lounge in the first floor library, a copy of Gloria Naylor's *Mama Day* opened across his chest, Coltrane's *A Love Supreme* playing softly in the background, telling himself he would one day have a place like this for his own.

The doorbell startled him, as the sound seemed to ring throughout every floor of the house all at once. He stirred, rolling himself off the chaise, and headed for the door. He wasn't expecting company—he didn't know anyone in New York—so he contemplated not answering the door. But wasn't the point of housesitting to let people know the house was being occupied? He reluctantly went to the door and pressed the intercom button.

"Yes?" he answered.

"Is Florence in?" a woman asked.

"She's out right now. I can take a message, though."

"I just came by to drop off a book I borrowed," the woman said.

"You can leave it with me, if you want."

"Who are *you*?"

"I'm Troy, her nephew. Can I ask who *you* are?"

"Eris."

Troy hesitated.

No way. It couldn't be. But he only knew of one person named Eris, and he thought he remembered seeing a picture of her in the house somewhere.

He nervously clicked the button to let her into the brownstone. Opening the second bolted door behind the front door, he watched in awe as Eris Perry walked into the room, a large coffee table book tucked under her arm. Troy wanted to smile nonchalantly, but his nerves got the better of him. He mentally settled on just trying to avoid coming off as wack.

"Hi, Eris," he said, unsure of what else to say.

She handed Troy the book, and he took it, examining the cover. It was a collection of nude photography by Marc Baptiste.

"So you like Marc Baptiste?" he asked.

"Yeah. He asked me to pose for his next book."

Troy couldn't believe what he was hearing. Eris Perry,

with her beautiful, flawless deep brown complexion and the most incredible legs since Tina Turner, would be posing nude for Marc Baptiste. He did his best not to stare at her body through her orange and gold cotton sundress and the light scarf that hung from her neck, but because of the large tinted sunglasses she was wearing, he couldn't tell if she noticed him trying not to steal a glance at her.

"I think you'd be a great model," he said.

The exhalation from her mouth was part laugh, part sigh, as she shook her head. "So when will Flo be back?"

"She's in Barcelona about to take a 14-day cruise. She should be back at the end of the month. I'm housesitting for her."

He realized he was telling her a lot, but at this point he would have told her his social security number had she asked. This was Eris Perry, after all.

"Well, just tell her I came by," she said.

"Hold on," he said. "I didn't get a chance to offer you something to drink. I want to make sure I'm being hospitable."

"Nah, I'm good. Just tell Flo I came by."

"Yeah. Okay," he said. "I will."

Troy could feel the moment quickly slipping away as she headed toward the door.

"Hold on, Eris," he said. His nerves were finally settling out and now he was left only with the remnants of embarrassment.

She turned around, and he was unsure if she was perturbed by his attempts at delaying her departure. "Yeah?"

"I'm sorry. Can we start over? I'm Troy Dobbs, and I just graduated from Ellison-Wright College in Atlanta, and this is my first time being here in New York on my own, and I don't know anyone here, and it's been real quiet this first week, and, well, you're the first person I have had a conversation with since I've been here. I'm not gonna lie to you and say that being around a movie star like you isn't intimidating on some level, but on the real, this is the best thing that has happened to me since I arrived, and I guess I'm just trying to make it last as long as I can."

Eris listened to his rambling introduction and nodded. "It's cool," she finally responded. "I guess I can get some tea, if you don't mind."

Troy sighed. "Thanks. I really appreciate it, Ms. Perry."

"Just call me Eris," she said. "Troy, right?"

"Yes," he said, smiling at the fact she remembered his name. "Right up this way," he said, ushering her up the stairs to the second floor kitchen.

Eris took a seat at the table just off from the kitchen, while Troy pulled down the box of Tazo tea Aunt Flo kept in a cabinet next to the stove.

"Ellison-Wright College, huh?" she said.

"Yep. I finished last month with a major in mass communications."

"What do you plan on doing with that?"

"I just got accepted to USC for film school, so I'll be headed out there in August."

She smiled. "A filmmaker? Okay."

The obvious thing for him to do would be to ask her to

be in one of his student films, but he fought the urge to come at her like that. From what little he knew about the costs associated with using a member of the Screen Actors Guild, he was unsure if that was even a possibility anyway. "So what are you working on these days?"

"I start shooting a new film in another month. Vancouver again," she responded.

"Must be nice," Troy said, setting the water kettle on the stove. "I think I've seen just about every movie you've been in."

"Thank you. But can I be straight up with you, Troy?"

"Sure."

"I don't really like to talk about work and all that stuff when I'm kicking back and chilling. All of my friends are good about this. Your aunt is one of my closest friends. She's been around the industry for a while and she's been like a mother figure to me since I moved to Brooklyn. She's definitely one of the people who helps keep things normal in my life."

Troy took down two mugs from the curio cabinet against the wall of the kitchen. "I had no idea my aunt was even cool like that."

"She's definitely cool like that."

"Okay. So movies are out. What is there to do around here? I've been to a few places, but I'm still branching out slowly," he said.

"This is New York. Honestly, you can do whatever you'd like."

"Well, what do *you* like to do?"

"Seriously?" she asked, biting her lower lip. "Probably walk down the street to the promenade and look across the East River. It's the best view of New York, bar none."

"So do you live in Brooklyn Heights?" Troy asked, pouring the water and then dropping in the tea bags. "Chai okay?"

"Sure. And no. I live in Fort Greene, but I like to come over here every other weekend for a change of scenery."

He placed the mugs on the table and sat down across from her. For a moment they sipped their teas in silence.

"I really appreciate your company," he said.

"No problem. I'm actually enjoying just chilling out."

"Well, if you ever want to come back by and hang out, I'm definitely available."

She laughed. "I'll keep that in mind."

When Eris finished her mug, she stood. "Well, it's been nice. I have to run."

Troy stood. "Yeah. I understand. It's been cool."

Eris nodded.

"Let me walk you out."

"Thanks," she responded, following him down the stairs.

Four hours later and Troy was still floored by the fact that he'd hosted Eris Perry in his aunt's brownstone. He had wanted to ask for her phone number, but didn't want to pressure her after things had gone so well. Plus, she knew how to reach him if she wanted to.

Troy had graduated from Coltrane to A Tribe Called Quest's *Beats, Rhymes and Life* album, with "1nce Again" looping on repeat. He tried to read more of his book, but he found his mind unable to sit still. Instead, he turned off the lights, reclined on the chaise lounge, and nodded off to the dopeness of the J. Dilla beat filling the room.

2

SOLO

The Twin Towers punctuated the Monday evening skyline, the financial district glowing like a cluster of stars against the purple and pinkish hues of the evening sky. Across to the left, the Statue of Liberty stood in the sparkling blackness of the East River, almost like a rocket preparing to shoot off of Ellis Island and up into the dusky stratosphere. Troy stared in awe, his right hand planted firmly in his pocket, his fingers dancing along the nine and seven of the keychain he purchased several months ago alongside his graduation robe.

The gourmet ice cream in his cup was beginning to melt, and he wondered whether his introverted nature would cause him to miss out on what could be a great vacation. He had gone to the tourist-centric places, but hung back in the shadows, hoping to blend in with the locals. There were just *so* many people, none of them friends, associates, or even people with whom he would consider exploring his surroundings. It was then that this one reality dawned on him as he stared out into the night sky: for there to be eight million people who populated the metropolitan area of New York City, he could not possibly feel any lonelier than he did at that moment.

He knew Eris probably would not come by the brownstone until after Aunt Flo returned, and he doubted he would cross paths with her on the promenade either. Not now anyway. She had been the only person with whom he had shared any meaningful moment, and he dreaded that he might have come off as a starfucker in how he gushed over her.

When he returned to the brownstone, he picked up the phone and called his parents.

His mother answered in her warm, inviting voice on the second ring.

"Hello?"

"Mom," Troy said, hoping that his voice did not sound too winy.

"How are you doing, baby? How is Brooklyn treating you?"

"It's nice. How are you and Dad?"

"Oh, we're just fine. Your father's in the den watching some action movie on HBO. You know how he gets when he's watching his movies."

"Yeah," Troy said.

If he had been home with his parents, he would have been watching that movie with his father. It was part of their ritual and one of the reasons he fell in love with movies in the first place. When Troy's father found out that he had been accepted to film school, the old man could not have been any prouder.

"Are you okay?" his mother asked. "You sound a little down."

He started to lie to her, but his loneliness wouldn't allow him to. "It's just slow. I don't really know anyone here, and there's only so much I can do by myself. It's like going to Busch Gardens alone on the Fourth of July. You know what I mean?"

"I see," she responded. "I'm sure you'll find someone to do things with. You've only been there for a week."

"Well, I did meet someone yesterday, but I doubt I'll hear from her again before I leave."

"Why do you say that?"

"Because she's famous, Mom."

"Is that one of Flo's friends?"

"Yes."

They sat quietly on the phone for a few seconds.

"So are you going to tell me or do I have to ask?" his mother said.

Troy chuckled, enjoying the fact that his mother was not one for suspense, very much unlike his father. "It was Eris Perry."

"Are you talking about Victoria from that movie with Denzel?"

"That's her."

Troy found it curiously ironic that his mother only referred to actors by the names of characters they had played in movies she liked—well, actors other than Denzel—when she actually knew the actors' real names.

"Well, did you ask her out?"

Troy laughed. "Are you serious, Mom? This is Eris Perry we're talking about. What would I look like asking her out on a date?"

"Like a man who's interested in getting to know her better."

Troy started to respond, but he realized that his mother actually had a point. He could have asked her out, and while she might have turned him down, at least he would have known whether the mental energy he spent analyzing the previous day was really worth the effort.

The bottom line was that he was scared to ask her out. He knew that—and his mother probably knew that, although she would never say it directly to his face.

"I tell you what. If I see her again, I'll be sure to ask her out," Troy said.

"You do that," his mother responded. "And you know, if you wanted to, you could always lock up the brownstone and come back home for the rest of the summer. We'd love to have you here."

"Thanks, Mom, but I want to make the most of this opportunity. I'll still have a few weeks when I get home before I head out to Los Angeles, though. Maybe when I get back, Dad can gas up the boat and we can all go out on the bay and do some crabbing."

"That sounds like a plan."

"Okay. And Mom? Don't worry about me. I'll be just

fine. Things have just been a little slow. That's all. I promise I'll get out and have an adventure tomorrow."

His mother's warm chuckle filled the phone, and he smiled.

"Well, I'm going to go and check on your father. I'll have him call you later this week."

"Sounds good."

Once Troy and his mother said goodbye, he took out the latest copies of *Time Out New York* and *The Village Voice*, the two periodicals Aunt Flo had told him to pick up when he arrived, and laid them down on the dining room table, side by side. He was determined to find activities to fill his week. There was no way he would allow himself to spend another week standing still.

By the time he lay down for bed, he made himself a promise that he would not allow his loneliness to affect the rest of his trip. He couldn't help being *alone*, but he realized that he did in fact have some control over whether or not he felt *lonely*.

3

HITTIN'

Shortly after six o'clock the following evening Troy walked into the lobby of the Ambassador Theater. Monday had been black, the show's weekly night off, but Tuesday night was in full effect. People stood in line in front of the ticket and will-call windows. He had heard about rush tickets for *Bring in 'da Noise, Bring in 'da Funk* being available for $20, which was a bargain when it came to Broadway show prices. He purchased his ticket, and with a little over half an hour to blow in the meantime, he stepped outside of the theater and walked down toward the corner of 49th Street and Broadway. The city shone brightly with lights and activity for blocks, skyscrapers towering overhead from every angle, billboards touting various fashion brands and Broadway shows.

Finding a nearby building, Troy leaned his back against its warm brick facade, crossed his arms, and watched the activity around him. He was just as much a tourist as the people who poured over the sidewalks like ants emerging from a stomped anthill, but the filmmaker part of his personality preferred to maintain a kind of detached distance, taking in the view as if it were on a theater screen.

A mother held the hand of her toddler son, pulling him along the sidewalk, his little white sneakers determined to keep up. Passing them from the other side of the sidewalk was an older man, his smooth mahogany skin belying his white beard, his Gatsby hat slanted over his Afroed crown. Behind the older man was an Emo girl with blue hair and three piercings spaced across her bottom lip. Each of the people who passed Troy had a distinct style, and he wished he had his camera with him at that moment to capture what he was seeing. Instead, the camera sat in his bag back in Brooklyn, useless to him.

"I thought I was the only one who liked to people watch," a voice said, easing up beside him.

Troy turned his head, struggling to determine who this woman dressed in a lightweight military style jacket and a relaxed baseball cap pulled down low on her head was.

"Oh wow!" he said, reaching out to hug Eris.

She hugged him back.

"What are *you* doing out here?" Troy asked. "I almost didn't recognize you."

"This is my incog-*negro* outfit," she said, laughing. "I'm just waiting for my show to start. I have a friend in a play over at the Longacre Theatre. Are you catching a play anywhere around here tonight?"

"I'm going to see *Bring in 'da Noise*. Have you seen it?"

"Three times," Eris said, smiling. "It's really good! I don't think Savion Glover is doing the show right now, though. It seems like I remember reading somewhere that Bakari Wilder is doing his part. Either way, it'll be a good show if you've never seen it."

Troy nodded, unable to conceal the giant smile on his face. "I didn't think I was ever going to see you again before I left."

"Well, New York is a smaller place than you'd think. I'm sure you would have seen me at some point."

"I don't know," he responded, "but I was kinda hoping that I would."

"Why's that?"

"I enjoyed your company on Sunday, and, well, I was hoping that maybe we could hang out some time." He exhaled deeply, proud of himself for getting out the words. At least he fulfilled his promise to his mother to ask out Eris if he saw her again.

She nibbled on her bottom lip as she considered his words. "What are you doing after your show?" she finally asked.

"Nothing. Just wandering around Time Square before heading back to Brooklyn, I guess."

Eris glanced at her watch. "Meet me on the bottom level of the Virgin Megastore down the street at ten. Okay?"

"Sure," Troy said, nodding so enthusiastically he feared he might give himself whiplash.

"I'll be in the bookstore section near the magazine rack."

"Okay. I'll definitely be there."

"All right. Well, I have to head over to the theater. It's on the next street over. I'll catch up with you a little later."

"Most definitely," Troy responded, still unable to believe that she had not shut him down completely.

When he returned to the Ambassador and took his seat in the balcony, he was still smiling hard when the lights dimmed and the spotlight struck the first tap dancer.

Troy emerged from the theater still buzzing from the show. He had no idea of what the show was about and was surprised to learn that it was a retelling of the history of African Americans in the United States done purely through tap dancing, singing, and poetry. He was so in awe at times by what he had seen that he vowed to return and see the show again before he left New York.

The warm night air greeted him when he stepped back onto the street, and the realization that he would soon see Eris caused his heartbeat to quicken.

Just yesterday he was feeling crushed beneath his loneliness, and now his body was wrapped in euphoric bliss.

He walked to the corner of 49th Street and began his trek down to the Virgin Megastore off of Broadway and 46th Street. Part of him wanted to run the three blocks, but he realized that he still had about twenty minutes and that was time and distance he could use to calm his nerves.

What would she want to do? Did it even matter? He was just happy to be in her company again.

For the briefest of moments he considered trying to find the Longacre Theater and meeting her when she came out of her show, but he didn't want to seem too eager. Plus, there was no guarantee she would come out of the theater through the main entrance or if she would take one of the side entrances used by the actors.

Instead, Troy walked the short distance to the Virgin Megastore, dodging the tourists who lined the streets, many of them standing completely still in the middle of the sidewalk, cameras pointed upward at various billboards. He pushed through the revolving doors to find an atrium full of music and people standing all around. Listening stations lined the walls and people held CDs to their faces as they nodded to the music coming from the huge black headphones cupping their ears. Troy quickly found the escalator and descended to the second floor.

More music and swag.

He continued on the escalator down to the third level. Off to his right were DVDs. Behind him, a movie theater. Straight ahead was a cafe, and off to his left was the bookstore with a magazine rack along the side wall. He considered going into the cafe and ordering a soda or something to calm his nerves, but he decided against it. With is luck, he might inadvertently burp from remnants of the carbonated water bubbling through his system, and that would be too difficult to recover from.

He walked into the bookstore section and began

perusing the aisles. Restless, he finally eased over to the magazine rack and picked up a copy of *Vibe*. Toni Braxton stood naked on the cover, a towel covering her lower region, her hand crossing her breasts. Troy glanced at the title of the magazine to make sure he hadn't picked up a copy of *Playboy* by accident. Man, Toni had gone sexy, he thought, as he fanned through the pages to see the other pictures of her.

He didn't know how long he had been standing there, but when he glanced at his watch and saw it was nearly 10:40, he began to get the sinking feeling that Eris might have stood him up. He figured she must have had a Sidekick or cell phone or something, but without the number, he could do nothing more than wait. Placing the magazine back on the rack, he told himself that he would wait until 11 before heading down to the 42nd Street train station and catching the 2/3 line back to Brooklyn Heights.

Troy walked around the bookstore slowly, doubling back on the magazine rack several times. Still no Eris.

As he wandered around through the aisles, he thought back to the first movie he had ever seen of Eris Perry. She had played in a teenybopper update of a Shakespeare play where she was the best friend of the white brunette lead. Such roles seemed to be popular as Hollywood's version of diversity often depicted black people as sidekicks to white people, usually stealing scenes with their sass and humor. Eris was good at this when she got started, but then she did a movie where she was cast as a twenty-something lawyer named Victoria who fell in love with her married boss, played by Denzel Washington. That movie put her on the map, and since then, she had been working steadily.

With the DVDs directly across from the book section, Troy contemplated walking over there and checking to see which of Eris's movies might be in stock, but he stopped himself. He didn't want to get caught up in the fact that she was famous, although it was difficult not to.

As he waited, he began to get restless. Eris was the one who told him to meet her in this part of the store. She was also the one who had come by Aunt Flo's brownstone the other day and spent nearly half an hour chatting with him. Surely, she wasn't going to stand him up. Was she?

When Troy's watch showed 11 p.m., he reluctantly made his way to the escalator and began to ascend to the second level and then the first level. As soon as he stepped off, he saw her entering the store through the revolving door.

"Troy, I'm so sorry!" she said, walking up to him and hugging him. "I got held up with my friend. How long have you been here?"

"Since 10," he said.

"You've been waiting here the entire time?"

"Yeah, but it's no big deal. I was checking out some books and some music," he said. Truthfully, he was just happy that she'd shown up.

"I'm sorry," she repeated. "Have you eaten?"

"Not yet."

"Well, let's go get something to eat. My treat," she said.

"It's the least I can do since you've been waiting here for a while."

"Sounds good to me," Troy responded.

As they walked outside and hopped in a cab, Troy had already forgiven her for showing up an hour late. The reality of the situation was that he was going out to dinner with Eris Perry at 11 p.m. on a Tuesday night in New York City. He couldn't have written a better script even if he tried.

4

FLAVA

Troy had never been to Murray Hill before, and the quaint Manhattan-esque resident brownstones blending with mom-and-pop businesses scattered throughout the neighborhood surprised him even more by having a restaurant that was still open. The cab had zoomed east and delivered them to the door of a small Italian restaurant nestled between two other businesses and tucked down a set of stone stairs. The entire ride over had taken less than ten minutes.

"Come on," she said, walking down the stairs and opening the door.

Troy, still in awe, rushed to keep up with her.

"This way," a young guy dressed in black said, escorting the two of the them to a table in the back corner of the restaurant.

The rugged red brick pattern across the wall gave the place the aura of a wealthy person's wine cellar. Candlelight flickered from the tabletops scattered across the small room, but the overhead light still provided a modest glow.

Eris navigated easily through the maze of tables and chairs, leaving Troy to believe this was one of her usual spots.

"Nice and cozy," Troy offered, after they took their seats.

"Yeah. I like it here."

He almost said, "Do you come here often," but he realized how horribly cliché that comment was and instead asked, "How was your friend's play?"

Eris smiled, and it felt to Troy like the room brightened a bit more. "It was nice. He did an amazing job! When I see plays like that, it makes me think about returning to the stage soon. I'd have to find the right play and set aside time to do it, though."

Troy didn't know why he had assumed Eris's friend was a woman, not that it should have mattered, he figured. Still, he could feel the dull ache of insecurity throbbing in his temples. He tried not to let his disappointment seep into the conversation. "I would love to see you in a play. I think you'd be great."

"Thank you, Troy."

The server returned to the table to take their orders, and Eris ordered a salad, while Troy ordered an appetizer of fried calamari.

When the server left, Eris continued. "So what did you think of *Bring in 'da Noise*?"

"Off the hook! I've never seen anything like it. To be

honest, I thought about tap dancing like it was some white girl 'chorus line' kind of thing. But these guys were raw. Straight up beasts! They took the game to a whole new level."

Eris nodded. "I'm glad you liked it. Last year Savion Glover won a Tony for choreography. That cast is so talented! I'm amazed they can do that show night after night."

"Yeah," Troy said, "it seems like it would take a lot out of you, physically and emotionally. I see why people keep going back to see it over and over."

"Guilty as charged," Eris said, raising her hand.

Troy looked at her as she spoke, trying to remove the idea of her being a famous actress from his head. She was just a cool woman sitting across the table from him. She put on her pants one leg at a time, right? It was not beyond belief that they would have shared interests, was it? He took a deep breath and told himself that if he wanted to get to know her better, he could not allow her fame to distract him from doing so.

Then it happened.

She sneezed.

It was light but distinctive. In fact, it sounded like a small animal blowing a miniature party favor. It was cute-sounding and funny at the same time, and when Eris covered her mouth bashfully, excusing herself, Troy understood that she was just a regular person with regular person idiosyncrasies, and he could feel a burden lift from his shoulders.

They continued conversing until the food arrived and then continued afterwards. She told him about how she started acting and how she one day wanted to direct. She worried about the small number of black women who were directing and how the industry was biased against older women. She pondered what that would mean for her career down the road. The fear of her future pushed her to do more films now, but she had to be careful to do roles that would mean something years from now and roles that would not set back the achievements of other black actresses. "It's more of a burden than you'd think. You want to hear something funny? I always wonder what someone like Ruby Dee would think of my role in a particular movie. I don't know why I do that. Ruby Dee will probably never watch most of my films, but I think she's amazing and I don't want her to one day finally see one of my films and think that I set black women back fifty years. I know that probably doesn't make much sense, does it?"

Troy found her insecurities endearing and felt relieved that she could confide these things to him so easily. "It makes sense, but I doubt you'd have anything to worry about. I'm sure she'd be proud of you."

Eris smiled and placed her hand on top of his. "I appreciate you saying that."

The feel of her hand touching his made him want to dance around the table, but he played it cool, keeping his hand as still as he could for as long as she wanted her hand to be there.

"So what do you like to do when you're not working?" he asked.

"You know, I would've said travel. That's what I would have said if you had asked me before things really picked up with my work. When I was younger, all I wanted to do was travel the world. I actually wrote in my diary that I wanted to go to at least one hundred countries!"

"Have you been to a hundred countries?"

"More than a hundred. And sadly, I have only been to ten or so where I was actually able to kick back and really take in the culture without being connected to some project or the promotion for some project." She paused as she considered her own words. "I guess it's like a monkey's paw kind of irony: you want to see the world, but you wind up seeing most of it from a suitcase and a hotel window."

Troy started to say that he understood, but he had never travel as extensively as she had and felt that he was ill-equipped to co-sign on her statement. Instead, he said, "You said traveling is what you would have said if I asked you back in the day, but I'm asking you right now. What do you like to do with your free time now that you're, well, who you are?"

She smiled. "I've learned that simplicity best suits me when I have down time. A good book and a fluffy pillow are heaven. Just being still, you know?"

On this, he did understand. "Do you have a favorite author?"

"Gloria Naylor. I will read anything that she writes."

"You've got to be kidding me!" Troy said, breaking out into a broad smile. "I'm reading *Mama Day* right now."

"For real? That's my favorite book. I even gave a copy of it to Flo."

"That must be the one I'm reading then," he responded, suddenly feeling the emotional distance between he and Eris become exponentially shorter. It was like by reading her book, he was allowed a glimpse into an intimate space in her world.

"You'll have to let me know what you think of it. It's a beautiful story of love and sacrifice and one of the few books I've read that actually made me break out a box of Kleenex."

"It's like that?"

She nodded.

"So you and my aunt must be pretty close if you gave her a copy of your favorite book," he said between bites of his food.

"She's one of my best friends." Eris allowed the words to hang in the air, giving them full gravity, which only made Troy more curious.

"How did you meet Aunt Flo? I have to admit I'm pretty surprised that the two of you even know each other."

Eris burst into laughter, lowering her face and covering her mouth with her hand. She laughed hard, rocking back in her seat, the corners of her eyes moistening. Troy stared on in befuddlement, having no idea of what he had said that would elicit this kind of response. Was she laughing at him or something he said? His insecurities emerged and thickened the air around him.

"I'm sorry," she finally managed. "It's just that I'm not used to someone saying 'Aunt Flo' about an actual person."

Troy shrugged his shoulders. "I don't get it."

"Well, you're a guy, so maybe you wouldn't. To a woman, Aunt Flo is a monthly visitor."

He thought about it for a second. Then he blurted out, "Oh, a period?"

In the moment he heard his voice and saw the huge, embarrassed smile on Eris's face, he realized that he had missed the cue to use discretion on the topic. He mumbled the words "Aunt Flo" to himself quietly, deciding then that he needed to have another name for his mother's sister. He reasoned that he would call her Flo when talking to Eris, as it was awkward for him to say Aunt Florence, a name that only put him in the mindset of *The Jeffersons* TV show and the sassy maid of the same name. Plus, the name Florence felt too formal for such a laid back and cool woman.

Eris inhaled deeply, her laughter petering out into light exhalations. "I met Flo about six years ago. At the time, she was married to Dante Wilbourne over at Viacom. We were at a party down in SoHo and were introduced by a mutual friend. Truth be told, I just thought she would be someone I knew in passing, but that night we were both wearing handbags by the same designer, so we got into a conversation about that. By the end of the night, we had moved on to talking about books and what it was like for each of us moving to New York from The South. We just hit it off.

"After that, we would get together for lunch sometimes, and I guess we just got to a point where we trusted each other. When her marriage to Dante was on the rocks, I did my best to be there for her. Then later on when I was going through a situation with this guy I was dating, and things were pretty ugly, she was there for me, helping *me* through it. We've been through a lot together, and she's one of the few people on this planet that I actually trust. She's like an older sister to me, and frankly, at this point in my life, I don't know what I'd do without her."

"Is that why you took me up on the tea this past Sunday?" Troy asked.

"You kind of put everything out there when I was leaving, and I thought to myself that you seemed like a nice enough guy to talk to for a few minutes. But I'm not gonna lie. If you had been anyone else's nephew, I probably would have kept it moving right along."

He nodded, for once appreciating his proximity to Flo, while feeling slightly deflated that her kindness was more the result of nepotism than his own charm.

Once the bill came, Troy offered to pay.

"I told you earlier. I got this," Eris said, sliding her hand around his and gripping the leather-encased bill.

"Well, thank you," he responded. "At least let me pick up the tip then."

Eris chuckled, her voice almost musical. "I take it you're not used to women paying for the meal."

"Truthfully? No."

"Well, sit back and enjoy it. I'm sure you'll be back to paying for meals in no time."

He laughed to himself. "Probably."

They walked outside into the warm night air, and Troy glanced down at his watch. It was almost 1 a.m., but he was not ready for the evening to end just yet. He waited for a moment to see what Eris wanted to do, and when she didn't say anything, he asked, "Feel like going for a walk?"

"Sure."

As they walked past the brownstones lining either side of the street, Troy began to wonder if this was in fact a date. It felt intimate and comfortable in the way that a date in Atlanta would have felt. The last date he had been on was a week before graduation and it was with another graduating senior named Beulah (a name he couldn't seem to match to her face). It was more of a "farewell/sorry we never hooked up in college" kind of date that ended with awkward, regrettable sex. Needless to say, he was still enjoying his evening with Eris and things were going ten times better than they did at the height of his date with Beulah.

"I can't see how Bad Boy is gonna survive without Biggie. You can't possibly mean that Puffy is gonna sell any records off his new album," Troy said.

"Puff is an entertainer, if ever there were one. Watch and see. He's probably gonna sell more records than any other artist on Bad Boy," Eris responded.

"But he can't rap!"

"I have a feeling that won't matter too much if his tracks are hot."

"Eris, as much as I want you to be right, I think you're overestimating him. He's a business guy, not a rapper. That album is gonna tank like the Exxon Valdez."

She laughed. "We'll see."

"You know," Troy said, pacing his steps to correspond evenly with hers, "this has been really cool—spending time with you."

Eris nodded. "You're not so bad yourself."

"Do you think maybe we could do this again—soon?"

"Okay."

At that moment, he reached for her hand and stopped her in her tracks. Standing beneath the overarching canopy of a small tree, he said, "I have a question to ask you. Is this a date?"

Eris chuckled and looked away, shrugging her shoulders. "Aren't we just hanging out? Two people enjoying each other's company."

"It feels like more. I know this is going to sound crazy, but I feel like I should kiss you right now."

"Oh, you do? What's giving you that vibe?"

"I don't know. *This. Here. Right now.* If this isn't a date, this would definitely be the best non-date of my life."

"You like to overthink things, don't you," Eris said, continuing to walk down the sidewalk.

Troy quickly caught up to her, now feeling slightly embarrassed. Was he supposed to have not said anything and just kiss her? He didn't know, but he was determined to find out.

He reached for her hand again, and when she turned to

face him, he leaned in and kissed her softly on her lips. She chuckled softly to herself, her eyes registering a mild surprise. For the life of him, he could not tell what she was thinking now that he had acted.

"That was nice," she finally said.

He leaned in to kiss her again, but she placed a hand on his chest, pushing him back. "Easy, Loverboy."

"Did I do something wrong?" he asked.

"No, but I think we need to call it an evening."

Troy waited for her to say she was just kidding. After all, they had only walked two blocks from the restaurant. Maybe he wasn't supposed to kiss her after all.

"Are you *sure* I didn't do something wrong?" he asked again.

"You're cool," she offered nonchalantly.

"Can I get your number and call you some time then?" he asked.

"Don't worry. I know how to contact you."

She stepped between two parked cars and lifted her hand, hailing a passing taxi. When the vehicle stopped, she looked back. "I enjoyed dinner."

"Yeah, it was nice."

Troy was stunned as Eris got into the cab and it rolled off into the night.

Standing there on the street with nothing but the muted sounds of the city around him, he wondered what had gone wrong. Why had she left him all alone on a dark street? She had picked him up, fed him, and dropped him off on the corner like a used-up, snot-filled rag, and while a part of him would have rejoiced in being a part of her world for the few hours of magic they shared, the other part of him felt betrayed, let down, and disappointed.

By the time he reached the train station and took a seat on the bench to wait indefinitely for the next train to come, he almost believed everything he had just experienced was a dream—a really bad dream—but he knew the truth: he was awake, in a tunnel below ground, and Eris, in all of her glorious splendor, was now gone.

5

PERSPECTIVES

*T*roy awoke, stretched out perpendicularly across his bed, the sun blazing through the room's blinds. He glanced at the digital clock on the nightstand, surprised to see that it was nearly 1 p.m. He could scarcely remember how he made it home. All he could make out was that he had waited nearly half an hour for the train and had fallen asleep on the ride home, nearly missing his stop. How he made it up the stairs to the his bedroom on the second floor of Flo's brownstone was beyond him.

As soon as he placed his feet on the floor and stood up, the thought of the dinner with Eris filled his head. It had all ended so weirdly. Even as he stumbled into the shower, he still had an "out of sync" feeling about all that had happened. He had totally misread her body language. Still, she had allowed him that first kiss. Maybe there was much more to it than she was willing to tell him.

Flo had a computer in one of the bedrooms that had

been converted into an office space, so Troy logged on to the Internet and went to Yahoo! to search for anything he could find on Eris. Mainly, he wanted to know if she was romantically involved with anyone. He didn't know if they put those kinds of things on the Internet, but he imagined it would be pretty cool if they did. When his search came up empty, save the few things about her films, he resigned himself to the fact that he would just have to let the situation play out on its own. Maybe she would call; maybe she wouldn't. Either way, he would have to be okay with that.

Once he had brushed his teeth and gotten dressed, he walked downstairs to the library, picked up the copy of *Mama Day* he had been reading, the one Eris had given Flo, and stretched out on the chaise lounge.

He had to stop and reread every other paragraph because his mind kept drifting. Was Eris thinking about last night like he was? What did she want from him? The dinner had been her idea. In fact, every major element of the time they had been around each other since they met she had overseen. Maybe he was just a temporary escape from the life she knew. Most of her friends and associates were probably connected to the entertainment industry. He was just a mass communications grad from a small black college in Atlanta, and for the moment, at least, he was unconnected to her world. He was just a guy on vacation taking in the beauty of New York.

Unable to still his mind, Troy stood up, tossing the book on the chaise. He returned to his bedroom and packed a notebook and camera into his backpack. He would just go exploring today, he figured. Grabbing his wallet and keys from the dresser beside the bed, he headed downstairs, locked up the brownstone, and started his trek across the Brooklyn Bridge into Manhattan.

"WHAT EXACTLY IS *CELEBRITY*?" TROY PONDERED, AS HE navigated the streets of the financial district. Was it the fact that your face and your art were ubiquitous to a particular population? Did it make those people really any different from people who did not have the same level of exposure? After all, celebrities were just doing their jobs, and it just so happened that those jobs were just more high profile than others. But if celebrities were just high profile workers, why did so many people clamor for fame or the chance to be scrutinized by the general populous? Maybe it had to do with money—or better yet the misperception that fame and wealth were conjoined. Just a glance at many of the rappers perpetuating the illusion of wealth because their record labels forced them to do a Hype Williams video was enough to make one wonder if there was some form of social security plan for the celebrity whose fame had expired before his bank account birthed a positive integer.

Troy cared increasingly less about Eris's *celebrity* and next to nothing about whether her talents had netted her a healthy income. All he knew was that he was becoming more enamored with her, the same as he would a sista he had been heavily scoping on the yard at Ellison-Wright.

This was a difficult notion to juxtapose with her awkward departure from the previous evening, though.

If he were to focus on everything from the moment he saw her on the corner of 49th and Broadway until the moment they walked out of the Italian restaurant, he would have slept soundly, blissfully even, but those last minutes were impossible to ignore. For every minute he sat in the bowels of the Metro station waiting for a train to come in the wee hours of the morning, he felt the compounding sting of her abrupt departure. Maybe the kiss was too much.

The kiss was probably too much.

But hadn't she kissed him back? And hadn't she said that it was nice? Wouldn't that have been an invitation to continue?

As Troy removed the SLR camera from his backpack and attached the zoom lens, it began to dawn on him that maybe he had not done anything wrong after all. Maybe Eris's conflicts were of a more ambivalent and personal nature and had little to do with him. Troy considered this for a moment, but it did not provide him the kind of relief he so desperately craved.

Pointing his camera at the Brooklyn Heights promenade, he began snapping shot after shot. From the other side of the East River, it was easy to think the entire view of things was Manhattan-centric. Seeing his neighborhood from Manhattan, however, provided him a fresher perspective. The view was different, low-key. Beautiful.

He could hardly make out the people on the promenade

and wondered briefly if perhaps Eris was walking along the brick path looking casually across the East River to where he stood. He would need binoculars, definitely something much stronger than his lens, to know if that were true, but he doubted it. After last night he was unsure of whether their paths would ever cross during his remaining weeks in Brooklyn.

It had been magical, yes. Brief and inviting? Yes. But was it destined to be more than an incredibly surreal, yet singular, occurrence? Probably not.

Once Troy finished taking pictures, he caught a train up to the Village, had a slice of pizza, and returned back to Flo's place, content to spend the rest of the afternoon reading and listening to music. He was, after all, on vacation, and he knew that USC would provide him with little time to rest in the fall.

6

HEAT

*A*s Troy climbed the steps of the brownstone, he noticed a folded sheet of paper taped to the front door. He quickly peeled it away and opened it.

Troy,

I was in the neighborhood and just dropped by to see if you were around. Call me when you get a minute. (718) 555-2235.

Eris

She had come back after all. And she had left him a phone number.

Troy had been mentally preparing himself to accept the fact that he would never see her again, except maybe on the big screen, but the note, in its beautiful cursive penmanship, begged to differ.

He examined the sheet of paper looking for a time. She might still be in the neighborhood, he thought, as he trotted down the stairs and over to the promenade. Had she really been there while his lens was pointed in this direction?

He scanned the length of the promenade looking for Eris and then for people who might have been Eris in disguise. The only people he saw, however, were the usual people from the neighborhood, the regulars who walked their dogs, jogged, or lazed about the benches daily.

He walked back around to Henry Street and headed for Montague, but once he reached the ice cream parlor there, he knew that he would never be able to find her among the hundreds of people scattered sporadically down the street going toward Fulton Street. He had simply missed her.

Still, there was the phone number, something that assured him that they would be able to reconnect regardless.

He trotted back to the brownstone, raced upstairs, and picked up the phone.

❧

THE PHONE RANG SEVERAL TIMES BEFORE ERIS answered.

"Troy?" she said.

He blushed at the thought that she had been anticipating his call to the point she would answer with his name.

"How did you know?" he said, more as a play of modesty than anything else.

"Flo's number is in my phone already. It came up on the screen."

Troy chuckled to cover his embarrassment, reminding himself that he was *still* on the phone talking to Eris—which had to be pretty damn spectacular, given the situation.

"I just got back to the house. When did you come through?" he asked.

"Oh, I passed through around noon. I was just in the neighborhood and decided to drop in and check on you."

She said it like she was doing Flo a favor and had no personal interest invested in the situation. Troy found this a bit difficult to believe, though.

"I hate that I missed you. It would have been nice seeing you again."

"Yeah," she said.

He could not tell if she was being nice or genuine.

"I'm free for the rest of the evening—if you wanted to hook up and hang out," he offered.

"Hold on," she said, stepping away from the phone.

He waited for nearly two minutes before she returned.

"Wanna go to this event with me tonight?" she asked. "It's a fashion show for Fila or something like that."

Troy grinned so widely that he felt his face aching from the stretch. "Sure. Just tell me when to be ready."

"The invite says seven, but I know the show won't start until closer to eight. I can have the car come by and get you around 6:30."

"But how should I dress?"

"It's a fashion show. Just wear something chill. There'll probably be a DJ, an open bar, and a lot industry people there. I'm wearing a designer tee, jeans, stilettos, and one of my bags."

"Oh," Troy said, suddenly realizing that this was the kind of event that was actually several levels above his present social station. There would be celebrities there, he knew, and with him arriving with Eris, he would need to really dig into his vault of confidence to pull this off. For a split second, he almost asked if he could bail out, but he knew she would never present him with the opportunity unless she really wanted him to go. He would just have to suck it up and pull himself together. "I'll be ready," he finally said.

"Okay. I'll see you then."

He hung up the phone and looked at the clock. It was nearly 4:00 p.m., definitely not a lot of time to calm his nerves.

He hopped in the shower and started brainstorming what he had in his suitcase that he could wear, since he didn't have enough time to go out and buy anything. By the time he dried off, he had pieced together his wardrobe in his head. He would wear a white dress shirt, a pair of dark, dressy denims, his black leather loafers and matching belt, and a navy blue blazer. While he didn't consider himself a fashion aficionado, he had learned at Ellison-Wright that there were core staples a man should always travel with, especially if he were gone for longer than a day. Of course, he had not intended to wear *that* particular combination at any point; still, he was pleasantly surprised such seemingly arbitrary advice could prove so instrumental in a bind like this.

He finished dressing around 5:30 and headed into the kitchen to grab a snack, just in case it was a while before he ate again. Then he went downstairs to wait in the library.

Looking around the quiet room, Troy could feel his pulse quickening. What if he said the wrong thing or did the wrong thing? It was one thing to do something foolish in the presence of Eris, but it was another thing to do something publicly that could embarrass both of them. The fact that they would be going together meant that, at least publicly, they were somewhat of a couple—if only for the evening. Last week if someone told him he would be escorting the most beautiful actress in Hollywood to a fashion show, he would have slapped the person who was doing the talking. No one dared dream that big!

Troy could see the Lincoln Town Car through the front window when it pulled up. He locked up the brownstone and walked down the steps. The car's windows were tinted, and by the time he pulled the handle of its door, his stomach was in knots. He looked into the car and immediately realized it was empty.

"Excuse me," Troy said in the direction of the driver. "Who sent this car?"

"Sir, my dispatcher sent me to this address. I'm supposed to pick you up and take you to 41st and 6th in the city. That's all I know."

Troy stared at the empty backseat, wondering where Eris was. Hadn't she said that she was coming to pick him up? Or had she said that she was sending a car to get him? He couldn't remember.

"Sir, are you getting in?" the driver asked. He was attempting to be polite, but it was clear that he was becoming annoyed with this kid who didn't seem to appreciate having a driver take him into the city.

"Yes," Troy responded, hopping into the backseat. So this was how it was going to play out, he thought, as the driver navigated the neighborhood then onto the Brooklyn Bridge.

Seeing New York City from a car was refreshing. The evening sun gave a golden tint to the buildings, and as the car sped along the streets, Troy noticed pedestrians moving about the sidewalks and sighed that he was not one of them. The plush comfort of the town car added to the fact that this was not just a taxi ride where plopping your behind in the seat cost $2.00—that is, if you were able to catch a cab as a black man.

The Town Car pulled up to a stop outside of a nondescript brick building, where a short line of people stood in line behind a red velvet rope. They were flashing passes and the bouncer was admitting them one by one. It was then that Troy realized he didn't have a pass.

"Excuse me," he said to the driver. "Did the person who sent this car for me leave a package with you to give me?"

"No, sir. No package. I was just told to drop you off here."

Troy stepped out of the car and walked toward the line. It was moving quickly, and he realized he would be face-to-face with the bouncer, empty-handed, in a matter of seconds. He quickly stepped out of line and walked to the pay phone on the corner, retrieved Eris's phone number, and called her.

His call went straight to voicemail. "Hey, Eris, I just wanted to let you know that I was here. I'm standing outside the club waiting for you. I don't have a cell phone, so I'll just be out front waiting." He hung up and walked back to the club.

A limousine pulled up in front of the building, and Z, a famous supermodel, stepped out and was quickly ushered through the door. Troy went back to the line behind the rope, trying to play it cool, although the June air was starting to make him sweat.

"Pass?" the bouncer said, holding out his hand to Troy once he'd reached the front of the line.

"I'm a guest of Eris Perry's," he said. "I might be on a list or something."

The bouncer, a huge Puerto Rican guy with muscles jumping through his black designer t-shirt, lowered his head, scanning the list. "What's your name?"

"Troy Dobbs."

The bouncer looked up and down the different pages of his clipboard before saying, "No Troy Dobbs on the list."

"What should I do? Eris Perry had a car drop me off here to meet her."

"Yeah, and Janet Jackson is giving me a ride home tonight," the bouncer said, laughing. "Step to the side, kid."

Troy stepped out of line, his face flush with embarrassment, his body sticky with sweat. He glanced at his watch. It was 7:15, and he figured surely Eris should know by now that he'd arrived. Frustrated, he walked across the street and leaned against the building facing the club.

Over the next ten minutes, Town Car after Town Car, limousine after limousine, pulled up dropping off a Who's Who list of celebrities at the front door. At a certain point Troy lost track of who was in the building, but he figured the list of famous people rivaled that of a major awards show. All he knew was that he was still outside, his blazer now resting in the crook of his arm, his dress shirt sleeves cuffed to his elbows. His feet were starting to hurt from standing so long in his loafers, and he contemplated just how much longer he would wait outside the club before walking down to the Metro Station a few blocks away and heading back to Brooklyn.

He glanced at his watch again. He would leave at 7:30, he told himself.

Once the long hand of his watch touched the numeral six, he took one last look at the door. Surely she would come to get him. It would have been pointless to have a car bring him this far just to drop him off and leave him. He turned to leave.

That's when he saw a thin woman with an Afro emerge from the club, wielding a Sidekick and looking frantically from left to right. It took a moment before she looked straight ahead in Troy's direction. He stood still, unsure of whether she was walking towards him or simply crossing the street.

"Troy?" she said.

"Yes."

"I'm Regina, Eris's assistant. We've been looking all over the place for you. Have you been out here the entire time?"

Troy reached up dramatically and wiped the sweat from his brow. "Yeah. I've been out here for a while. I was actually just about to leave."

"Don't do that. Come with me. The show hasn't started yet. Eris has been waiting on you since seven."

Troy sighed and considered telling Regina that he'd pass. He was tired and felt sticky. His coolness had expired the moment he had to take off his jacket and cuff his sleeves.

"I'm really sorry," Regina added. "Things got mixed up. I only knew to come out here because we called the car service, and they said that you had already been dropped off."

Troy looked around him, noting that all of the activity was straight ahead. The party was directly in front of him, and he already knew the myriad of entertainers in the building because he had seen them all arrive. It was definitely tempting. But he realized all of that paled in comparison to the fact that Eris had been waiting on him, refusing to stop looking for him when he didn't arrive. Although the situation had been horribly inconvenient, one thing seemed clear, as far as Troy was concerned: Eris actually cared about him.

He looked into Regina's expectant eyes and nodded. "Okay. Let's go."

Regina smiled and walked back to the bouncer.

"He's with Eris Perry," she said to the bouncer, pointing at Troy, whose clothes were damp with sweat.

Troy did his best to be cool and nod his head like, "I told you so."

The bouncer looked at Troy and said, "Oh word? My bad, my man." He then stepped aside and let Regina and Troy into the building.

Behind Troy he could see that the sun was starting to set.

7

CHOICES

Regina handed him a paper napkin from her purse without saying a word. This only amplified how humiliated Troy was that he had to stand outside long enough to sweat through most of what he was wearing. The air conditioning inside the club was a welcome reprieve, and once he wiped his brow with the napkin, he realized that he would probably be dry by the time the show ended.

Regina led him through the throng of A, B, and C-listers. Supermodel Z was chatting with Puffy, while Isaac Hayes escorted his date to a seat near the stage. When Troy got within range of Eris, his heart melted like a popsicle lying on a Mississippi sidewalk in July. This was the first time he had seen her really looking like the *movie star* Eris Perry.

Eris was famous for a particular bob hairstyle, where her hair was faded in the back. The cut was so connected to her image, it was often referred to as the Eris Perry cut, in the way the Halle Berry's hairstyle was referred to as the Halle Berry cut. With the makeup and that glow of celebrity, Eris looked different than she had when Troy had hung out with her days before. She had been low key with the hats and loose clothing, but now this was Eris Perry in all of her famed glory. The sight of her put Troy in so much awe that if he died at that moment, he would have sailed into the great beyond a very satisfied man.

When Eris noticed Troy approaching, her lips gave way to a smile. She was smiling for *him*, Troy thought, unable to hide his own smile. She stood and embraced him.

"I'm so glad Regina was able to find you. I was starting to get worried that the car service had broken down or something."

He started to recap the last forty-five minutes of standing outside getting dissed by the bouncer in the hot June sun, but then he decided to let it go. After all, she had just embraced his damp body and not commented on it. She knew, just like he knew, that everything that had happened was unfortunate, and her willingness to move forward with the evening inspired him to do the same.

"It was an adventure—but I made it. Just in time." He smiled so she would know there were no hard feelings.

"I see you met my assistant, Regina."

"Yeah. She's cool people."

Regina took a seat on the other side of Eris, leaving Eris and Troy to converse privately.

"I'm just glad to be here with you," Troy said, taking in all of her beauty up close.

She reached out and squeezed his hand. "I just hope you enjoy the show."

"I'm sure I will."

The lights dimmed and the runway lit up with model after model walking the runway wearing the latest in the fall sport collection of Fila, a brand that Troy had once enjoyed as a child, particularly when it was an Italian import. From what he was hearing, though, there were some trademark issues and now there was a rebranding of the U.S. version. He half-expected Z to model in the show, but she was clearly a supermodel and in attendance primarily as a celebrity, which was further enhanced by the fact that she sat next to Puffy.

Troy found it difficult to really pay attention to the models on the runway. All he thought about was what would it be like to have a space like this to himself with Eris. She was the model walking through the runway of his mind, and truth be told, it did not matter what label she was wearing or from what collection.

The fashion show didn't last long, and within minutes the DJ had started spinning tunes for those who wished to remain afterwards. Many of the celebrities were already at the coat check, preparing to leave for other events. Eris leaned over and whispered something to Regina, who nodded and walked away. Eris then approached Troy.

"So what did you think of the show?" she asked.

"Pretty cool. Thanks for bringing me."

"No problem. I'm just sorry you had to wait outside so long." She patted his chest. "But at least now you're dry," she said, chuckling.

He allowed himself to smile, silently appreciating the fact that his shirt was no longer sticking to him.

The DJ started playing "Runnin'" by Pharcyde, and Troy found himself involuntarily nodding to the rhythm of the music.

"You wanna dance?" Eris asked.

"Are you serious?"

"Or are Ellison-Wright men too good to dance?"

Troy laughed, taking her hand and guiding her onto the dance floor, where several other celebrities and socialites had already gathered to dance. He loved the song and found himself rapping along with it. Eris smiled, watching him as he moved from side to side, matching him with her own smooth movements.

The DJ mixed in several other songs, and they continued dancing, but when Troy felt the first beads of sweat forming on his forehead, he slowed down to a basic two-step. There was no way he would allow himself to sweat through his clothes a second time.

"What do you have planned for the rest of the evening?" Troy asked.

"I don't know. What's up?"

"I was just hoping the evening wouldn't have end here."

Eris smiled. "You don't hold back, do you?"

"What do you mean?"

"You're pretty straight forward with what you want."

Troy shrugged his shoulders. "I don't know. I guess it always feels like it might be the last time I see you whenever we're together, so I want to at least put it out there for you so you'd never be able to say you didn't know what I was thinking."

"I can appreciate that. Let's go."

Troy didn't even bother to ask where. He would have gone anywhere she asked him to go.

THE TOWN CAR DROPPED THEM OFF ON 6TH AVENUE, near 30 Rockefeller Plaza. Troy thought it an odd choice, given the general popularity of the location, but he was happy to be in such a beautiful architectural space with Eris.

They walked between skyscrapers toward the overlook, where flags surrounded a courtyard that would serve as an ice skating rink in the winter. They took a seat on one of the benches between the two buildings situated just behind the overlook.

"When I first moved to New York, I came here," Eris said. "There were hundreds of people walking around here and down there in the courtyard." She pointed just beyond them at the pit that lay ahead, all of the tourist activity taking place on a lower structural level. "You know, people told me that I would never make it in the industry living in New York. 'You have to move to L.A.,' they kept saying. But I've always been in love with this city—ever since I was a little girl and used to see it on TV."

Troy nodded. "You're from Louisiana, right?"

Ellis smiled, nodding. "Small place called Monroe, somewhere along I-20 between Mississippi and Texas."

"When did you come here?"

"As soon as I graduated from high school. There was only so much I could do at home. Booking local commercials and doing community theater got kind of old after a while. My mom thought I was crazy for coming here. She wanted me to go to Xavier University in New Orleans and major in biology or something. I swear I thought she would disown me when I turned down the scholarship offers for school. In the end, it was my dad who convinced her that I could just defer for a year and see what happened with my acting. I think they both figured the 'real world' would shock me back into school faster than Flo Jo doing 100 meters, but they were wrong. I had no intention of ever going back—not if I could help it."

"So how long have you been in New York?" Troy asked.

"Long enough."

"Seriously. How long?"

"Going on fifteen years," she said, chuckling. "I guess that's long enough for me to know that I probably won't be going to college."

Troy quickly surmised that Eris was around thirty-three-years-old. Being that he was only twenty-two, the idea of the eleven year age difference was both jarring and exciting.

"I know what you're thinking. I see you over there doing the math. You're trying to guess my age."

"No, it didn't even cross my mind," he lied.

"Most women in the industry are really funny about their ages. The way I see it, if you hide things like that, they'll probably come to light even faster. And with this Internet thing, it's probably just a matter of time before people start putting other people's business out there for the world to see. I doubt Ruby Dee or Bea Richards ever had to think about those kinds of things."

Troy nodded. "You mentioned Ruby Dee before. I take it you're a big fan of older actresses."

"I guess you could say that. In those older films, like *A Raisin in the Sun* and *Stormy Weather*, those women were classy and talented. Not to say that sisters aren't doing it well now, but it was just different back then, I guess. There was a lot more on the line." She paused. "Maybe I'm just romanticizing the past, but it just feels like those women were doing more than just acting. That's what I try to remind myself when I take a job: what I'm doing is bigger than just memorizing lines and saying them in front of a camera. The right role could change a life. I truly believe that."

Troy smiled awkwardly. "I guess I never really thought of it that way."

"When you finish film school, you'll probably make your own films. At first you'll probably be happy to be making films and getting paid to do it, but I imagine at some point you're going to give a lot of thought to what you want your art to say to people."

"Probably so," he responded. "So have you met any of the women you admire?"

Eris broke into a broad smile. "I actually met Ruby Dee once. It was at an NAACP banquet. I was too through! So much the fan that night! I even got my picture taken with her. I have it on my bedroom dresser. You know how you expect a person to be a certain way and it turns out that they are even more amazing than you originally thought? Well, that's Ruby Dee. I just love her to death!"

"Are you still in touch with her?"

"No. I only saw her that once—and to tell the truth, I'm not sure I would know what to say to her if I had to speak to her again. She leaves me completely speechless."

Troy smiled as he considered that someone as famous as Eris Perry could be that in awe of another actress. "That's really cool, your being a fan of someone like that. I didn't think famous people were fans of other famous people like that."

Her eyes still dancing from the memory of her encounter with Ruby Dee, Eris said, "We're all human beings, and human beings are always in awe of other human beings."

"Fair enough."

They sat staring at the glowing lights that illuminated the building in front of them, just beyond the overlook. Businesses lined the streets on either side, and the lights that illuminated everything around them were strong enough that he could have photographed the space around them as clearly as if it had been day.

Apropos of nothing, Troy said, "I haven't been able to stop thinking about you since you came by the brownstone on Sunday. This has all been so surreal. I'm still adjusting to being here with you."

Eris stretched out her arms and gazed up into the night sky. "I don't know why, but I feel like you're a really cool guy, and I guess that's why I asked you to come out with me again after what happened the other night. It's just hard for me, though. Some times I can't tell if a guy is really into me or if he's into who he thinks I am from the movies. That's the double edged sword of being well-known."

"I'm not gonna lie and say it never crossed my mind that you were Eris Perry, but being around you has shown me a very different side of you. I feel like I can tell you pretty much anything. When I got here this summer, I didn't know anybody, and then you came along and now I don't feel so—alone."

Eris placed her hand on his. "I know what you mean."

Troy lifted her hand to his lips and kissed it softly. She smiled in return.

"So," Eris said, "tell me about Ellison-Wright. Did you like it?"

Smiling, Troy told her about how Ellison-Wright was on the shortlist of colleges he had considered attending and how the deciding factor for him to go there was the fact that they had offered him a full academic scholarship—that and the mass communications program was among the best in the South. He talked about his freshman dorm and about later moving off-campus into a hotel downtown that had been converted into a co-ed dormitory. He talked about what it was like to pledge a fraternity during his junior year and even what it was like falling in and out of love in college.

"It all sounds amazing," Eris responded, once he had finished. "The closest I've come to college is playing a college student on television. But I keep wondering about what I missed out on when I came here."

"But if you had gone to school, you wouldn't be sitting here with me right now. I just believe that the decisions we make guide us to a singular result," he said.

"Something you learned in college?"

"Not really. Just something I believe about the way the world works. You had to bring that book by Aunt Flo's place at that exact time on that exact day for our paths to cross."

"So it's like fate or something?"

"In a way, yes."

His eyes met Eris's and they locked on each other, unflinching. For the first time since they met, he felt they were actually *seeing* each other, unguarded and honest.

"You're beautiful," he said.

She looked at him for a moment and then leaned in, kissing him deeply. He yielded to her touch, and in their cocoon of solitude, shielded from the stray tourists wandering down Sixth Avenue or down in the courtyard, Troy allowed his heart to rejoice in the moment.

ERIS CALLED REGINA AND HAD HER ARRANGE FOR A

car to come and pick them up and take them back to Brooklyn. While they waited, Troy taught her how to play the "movie" game, something he and his classmates did for shits and giggles on Friday nights to blow off steam from the week's classes. The rules, as he explained them to her, were to not just say the lines from a movie, but to *deliver* them in the way the original actor had done. When the other person guessed the movie, then that person got to select and perform a new line. This was the first time Troy had ever played the game with a person who was actually in movies, though, so the game was that much more interesting.

Troy started the game off with a line from *The Color Purple.*

"Uh, you had her yo way—and I had her mine—but we both had her!"

"Danny Glover at the kitchen table with Shug's husband, right?"

"Yep," he said. "Your turn."

"My mama used to say ta me, 'Fleet—FLEET?—That's my name: Fleetwood Coupe de Ville. Mama had high ideals, y'know what I mean?'"

Troy doubled over laughing. "That's the lion from *The Wiz.* Okay, here's a hard one: 'I wanna hate you. I wake up every morning wanting to tell you to go to hell, but I don't. I guess you got a hold on me like that.'"

"Really?" Eris said, smiling. "Is that your best impression of me?"

"I can't do the lines justice like you did. That was so

classic! I remember the first time I saw you in that scene with Denzel and how I thought to myself that he was the luckiest man on earth. He had a woman like you loving him."

"My character was supposed to be despicable—at least that's the way she was written in earlier drafts—but they changed the script a bit before production and made my character a little more complex. I'm glad for that. I doubt anyone would even remember that role if they hadn't."

"I went to see that movie three times, just to hear you say those words."

"Three times? Really? I think I've only seen the final version of the movie once. But I'm glad you enjoyed it."

He reached for her hand and felt her fingers interlock with his. "I know the car is on the way, but I wanted to ask you favor."

"What?" Eris said, looking a bit surprised.

"I want you to stay with me tonight," he said, then quickly added, "We don't have to sleep together. I just wanted enjoy your company until I fell asleep."

"Whoa, that's quite a request to lay on me. We've only been out twice, and to be honest, there's still a whole lot that I don't know about you. If we're gonna hang out, we need to take it real slow. I have to be careful because the level of trust I have to have before I go there with a man has to be strong enough to get over my fear that he would turn around and sell a story to *The Enquirer*."

"What happened there? With *The Enquirer* thing?" Troy asked.

Eris sighed, as if she were unsure she wanted to go into the details. "I was dating this guy named Leighton," she finally said. "I met him at a record store in The Village. This was a little over three years ago. He played in this Afro-Punk band, and I just thought he was really something special. He said all the right things and did all the right things. We took in the city together. He wrote songs for me. I would even run my lines with him. That's how close we were. And although we'd only been together roughly a year, I was starting to see the possibilities of something more long term. I had even considered having him move into my place. When you love someone that much, you don't think anything of when they snap random pictures of you around the house while you're lounging in your underwear or getting out of the shower. I knew he did photography on the side, but I thought it was more like a jack-of-all-trades artist thing, kinda like when Miles Davis started painting. I wouldn't have thought in a million years that he would turn around and sell those pictures to a tabloid. I thank God that I wasn't actually naked in any of them!

"But it wasn't so much that they tried to concoct a story around his pictures as it was that he betrayed my trust. I would have done anything for that man, and to think he cared so little about my feelings—about me—that he'd go behind my back and do that to me hurt me more than anyone will ever know. The only person who really knows what I went through with Leighton is Flo. She was there helping me to get out of the funk I was in. I was so depressed and felt like I couldn't trust anyone, but Flo wouldn't give up on me.

"I remember one day she came over to my place and I was buried under a quilt on my couch, cartons of ice cream and all kinds of shit lying around the room, my curtains drawn tight, blocking out all of the light. She rang the doorbell for fifteen minutes, until I finally crawled out from under the quilt to answer the door. She came in and turned on the lights and started fixing up my place. She reminded me of what happened with Dante Wilbourne, how he had cheated on her with all of those rap video prostitutes, and told me that I had to pull my shit together, how I couldn't roll over and play dead just because some man did something to hurt me. She refused to give up on me.

"I think that's why we're as close as we are, because up until then, she was my friend, but after Leighton, she became my big sister, or the closest thing I ever had to one."

Troy didn't know what to say as he listened to her. He had been heartbroken while he was at Ellison-Wright, particularly when he was pledging his fraternity and his girlfriend at the time had dumped him, claiming it was impossible for them to fix their relationship when he was pledging and had so little time for her. All he had was his line brothers to help him through that time in his life, and his heart went out to Eris because she had had to deal with that type of situation, too.

"For whatever it's worth," he said, rubbing her hand, "I'd never hurt you like that. I've been through that experience, and I wouldn't wish it on anyone."

She squeezed his hand gently.

"What *do* you really want from me?" she asked, her voice quiet and serious.

"Just to enjoy your company. Yes, I'm seriously feeling you, but you're also the only real friend I have here—and I like that. I love hearing your voice, seeing your face, feeling the softness of your lips against mine. I know you have a life and all and that this is just another week in your life, but to me this is the illest moment in my life, bar none. I'm wide open like James Evans's nostrils."

She chuckled and then leaned over kissing Troy lightly. "Do me a favor. Don't assume what I'm thinking. You don't know if this is just another week in my life or not. If this was all just some trivial stuff, I would not be spending my time with you. I don't think cither one of us has time to play games."

Troy nodded. "My bad. You're right."

The Town Car Regina called for earlier pulled up to the curb a few feet away from them. They hopped in.

"Where to?" the driver asked.

"Brooklyn Heights," Troy responded.

For the first few blocks, both he and Eris sat in silence.

"Is everything all right?" he finally asked quietly.

Eris looked at him and smiled. "Just thinking."

"Thinking about what?"

"About whether or not I'm gonna go home with you."

Troy was unable to conceal the huge smile growing across his face. "What can I do to help you make up your mind?"

"I don't know. I guess it's just a matter of trusting you."

"Well, what can I do to make you trust me?" he said.

"I just need some time to think."

As the car drove onto the Brooklyn Bridge, Troy could see the abyss of darkness resting between the two boroughs. The East River was out there somewhere, beside and beneath them, and soon they would be on the other side of the bridge, in Brooklyn, minutes from the brownstone. Eris still had not said anything to him or the driver about her intentions.

The car seemed to move quickly through the Brooklyn Heights neighborhood, and Troy silently wished the driver would slow down to a creep—just until he knew what Eris had planned to do.

The Town Car pulled up in front of the brownstone, and Troy opened his door, which was facing the curb. Once he stood up, he noticed that Eris had not moved.

He extended his hand to her. "Please come with me."

She looked at his hand for a moment, the car idling in the darkness of the street. "Don't make me regret this," she said, taking his hand.

Once they walked up the steps of the brownstone, Troy looked back. The car was already gone, and Eris had chosen him.

TRUST

Eris took a seat on Troy's bed and kicked off her heels, while he stood in the corner hanging up his blazer.

"I need to hop in the shower. I sweated my ass off earlier, and I don't want to have you talking about how funky I am," he said.

Eris chuckled, while looking around the room and taking in Aunt Flo's interior decorating.

When he saw that she was caught up in the layout of the bedroom, the Ernie Barnes prints on the walls and the various African American collectibles situated around the room, he added, "You're welcome to join me." He meant it in jest, but when he saw the surprised expression on her face, he backpedaled. "I'm just joking."

"Whatever. You know that was a real invitation," she responded, needling him.

"I was just saying something."

"Well, I think I'll be just fine. You can do this one by yourself," she said playfully.

"I'll be back in a few minutes. Just make yourself comfortable."

Troy left Eris stretched across the bed, thumbing through the copy of *Mama Day* he had brought up earlier from the library, while he walked down the hall to hop in the shower.

As he stood beneath the blast of water from the shower head, he wondered what Eris was doing while he cleaned himself. She had agreed to stay with him for the night, so he tried to interpret exactly what that meant to her. In college if a woman slept over at his apartment, that meant something was definitely going down on the sex tip. Just from Eris's mannerisms he knew that she viewed the situation a bit differently. She would kiss him and do things to show she liked him, but there was clearly a line that she was choosing not to cross at this point. As he pondered this, he realized that she was much more than someone to whom he was physically attracted; she was a friend. He loved talking to her, and he realized that was hardly a poor consolation should she not kiss him again that evening.

Once he finished showering, he tossed on the mesh basketball shorts he used as pajamas and a loose fitting t-shirt. There was nothing impressive about what he slept in, but he doubted he needed to be impressive given the fact that he would not be seducing her then. If she had decided to join him in the shower, that would have been another story. But she hadn't.

Troy entered the bedroom to find Eris stretched across the bed in one of his extra-large t-shirts and little else. The book was open in front of her as she lay on her stomach facing the direction of the pillows. From this angle, he could see the smoothness of the backs of her shapely legs extending from beneath the t-shirt and the rise of her ass like a gorgeous Georgia hill stretching the cotton fabric above it. The visual of her lying there in his clothing was beyond arousing, and he found himself stiffening under the mesh of his basketball shorts.

"Hey," he said. "I'm really feeling your change of clothes."

"Well, I needed something to sleep in, so I hope you don't mind that I grabbed one of your t-shirts out the dresser."

"Not at all. I'm not gonna lie, though. You look sexy as hell in that shirt."

Eris smiled, rolling over and scooting to the edge of the bed closest to him. "So you have me here. Now what?"

"You mean it's really that simple?"

"What do you mean?" she asked.

"Just tell you what I want to do?"

"Surprise me," she said.

"Well—" he started.

"Just don't say what I think you're gonna say. Be more original than that."

"But how do you know what I'm gonna say?"

"You're a guy."

"That's cold—and it's a stereotype on top of that," Troy said, laughing.

"So you weren't gonna say that you wanted to have sex with me?"

"Huh?" he responded, blushing. "What do you mean?"

"You heard me."

"Why? Would that have been so wrong, I mean given the circumstances?"

Eris stood up and approached him, pointing a finger softly into his chest. "*You* told me that you wanted to fall asleep talking to me. That's all you said. So, Troy, you should probably get to talking."

Her mannerisms were entirely coy, and he sensed she was a few seconds away from flat-out seducing him. Still, he marveled at her control of the environment. Everything was completely subject to her authority, and he loved every moment of it.

"I'm glad you're here," he said. "I guess I should start with that."

"Okay."

"And I had a wonderful evening."

"So far?"

"So far," he repeated. "And I can't stop thinking about kissing you."

He lifted her chin so that their lips met, and he savored the smooth, free movements of her tongue against his. He could feel her fingernails gently caressing the back of his neck and the warmth of her body pressing itself steadily against his.

She lifted her head, allowing him full access to her neck, and as he traced his kisses along her nape, he could feel her breath in soft, staccato exhalations, tickling his skin.

"Troy," she whispered. "As much as I like this, I just have to tell you one thing. I don't want to have sex with you tonight. Is that going to be a problem?"

With the persistent throbbing of his erection, pressed against her stomach through the fabric of her t-shirt and his basketball shorts, he felt the sting of disappointment. "It's cool," he allowed himself to say, before adding, "but why?"

"Try to see it from my perspective. I just met you, and I like you. But I don't want to move too fast with this. And you'll be gone in a few weeks anyway. I'm not into one night stands or selling myself short just because I'm attracted to a guy."

"I'm only going to L.A. That's like a second home to you, right? Hollywood and all."

"It doesn't work like that. I shoot in various locations, and when I'm working, I'm working. When I'm not, I live here in Brooklyn. My work and private lives are separate. I told you that when we first met."

Troy could feel the conversation pushing both of them out of the moment. There would be plenty of time to talk about their future together and how they would be able to continue building something, despite the distance. Right now, however, he could only focus on the feel of her body's warmth against him. He quickly kissed her again and sighed with relief when she placed her hand on his chest and caressed it.

"Hold on," Troy said, reaching over and dimming the lights in the room for atmospheric effect.

They found their way onto the bed and lay side by side, kissing each other. She eased off his shirt and he took off hers, and within moments the only things separating their bodies were their underwear. Troy reached for her panties and begin to pull them down, when she stopped him.

"I told you that I can't do that."

"We don't have to do that," he responded.

"Nothing good would come of us being completely naked in this bed. Trust me."

"I want you so badly right now. Are you telling me that you don't want me right here, right now?"

"It's not about what my body wants at this moment. It's about what my heart and mind will be able to live with in the morning," Eris said.

"I understand," Troy said, although being so close to her like this was killing him. "Wait. I have an idea."

"What?"

"Take off your panties."

"Troy, come on."

"Seriously. I won't touch you. Trust me. I'll do the same."

"Well, now I know I won't be doing that then," she responded.

"Please. Just trust me."

"First, tell me what you you have planned."

Troy sat up in the bed, resting on his elbows and looked into Eris's face. He could barely make it out from the thin veil of light that slid through the wooden blinds over the window and the dull glow coming from the nearby lamp.

"We'll lie down back-to-back, completely naked. But we won't touch. You will know that I'm not wearing anything, and I will know that you're not wearing anything either. We'll be close enough to feel the body heat of the other, but not close enough to actually be touching."

"And?"

"And then you will touch yourself, and I will touch myself, and then we can hear each other breathing and fantasize about being with the other person, and you can hear my voice, and I can hear your voice."

Eris started to chuckle softly. "How in the world did you come up with that idea?"

"It was the only thing I could think of that would allow us to be together without *being* together, if you know what I mean."

"That's just going to make me want you more," she said.

"Maybe, but at least you can have a release without the guilt of actually having sex."

He could see her shaking her head in disbelief. "That sounds so crazy."

"Hey it's just a thought, and I can't even say it's the best thought. But at least it's something," he said.

Eris was silent as she considered this. Her body body was so still she resembled a statue. Inside, Troy ached with anticipation.

"Okay. Turn your back," she finally said.

He quickly and nervously complied.

"I'm taking off my panties now."

Troy could feel her body shifting in the bed behind him and feel the covers move as she lifted her hand and placed her underwear on the dresser.

"Your turn," she said.

Troy quickly slid out of his underwear and lay anxiously facing the wall, the faintest bit of her body heat inches from his skin. "How do I know you're really naked," he said.

Eris grabbed his hand and placed it on her bare hip. Once he felt the warmth and smoothness of her skin, he took her hand and placed it on his hip.

"Okay. No more touching from this point forward," Eris said.

"Sure," Troy said, feeling the overwhelming nervousness of the moment.

They began slowly and in silence, their hands moving in cautious, deliberate rhythms, the thin sheet of the bed rising and falling with each movement, their voices punctuating the space with occasional moans of self-gratification.

Then Eris spoke.

"Troy, tell me what you're doing to me right now," she said, her voice a raspy whisper. It was the voice of a person who had been on the phone for hours with a lover and was approaching the climax of conversational intimacy.

Troy was suddenly pulled from his thoughts and was now being welcomed into Eris's fantasy. While the idea of what she was doing excited him even more, he worried that he might say the wrong thing and kill her flow. He offered, "I'm planting kisses along your stomach and onto your hips.

Can you feel my tongue, moist against your inner thighs?" He knew he was struggling. He would have rather spoken with his actions than his words, but she was leaving him little choice in the matter.

"How do I taste?" she said between moans.

"Incredible," he responded. "You are all that I want."

And then they fell silent again, and their voices were replaced with Eris's legs working furiously against the bed, struggling to gain traction on the damp sheets. Troy could only imagine what she looked like enveloped in the ecstasy of orgasm. He found himself so fascinated with his thoughts of her movements that he stopped touching himself and focused all of his attention on the violent shudder of her body and the crescendoing moan that rose in her throat, a primal melody, and filled the room like a tropical rain cloud bursting and releasing its storm down on the myriad of trees below.

When she climaxed, she backed up into him, her naked body moist with perspiration sliding wickedly against his. The touch of her warm, wet skin was electric, and Troy could not resist the urge to touch himself again and lose himself in the moment, climaxing shortly afterwards.

They lay side by side, the silence of the room attacked by the percussion of their breathing.

"Damn, I'm gonna need another shower again," he said jokingly.

Eris chuckled, running her hand across her flat stomach, the definition of her abs appearing with the exhalation of each breath. "I know I definitely need one at this point."

"So will you join me *now*?" Troy asked. He figured it was worth another try, although he kept his expectations modest.

"As long as you remember our arrangement," she responded, sitting up in the bed and brushing her hair from her damp cheeks.

Smiling, and quietly brimming with confidence, Troy walked down the hall and started up the shower again. This time Eris would be joining him.

They took their time bathing each other, and Troy absorbed each of her body parts with his eyes and hands, memorizing every centimeter of her skin, the ease of her smile, the curve of her body, the way her hair hugged her face in the moisture of the bathroom, that dimpled smile, those phenomenal legs, even the delicateness of her hands and feet, all for posterity. But her eyes were what really took away his ability to think clearly. Her eyes were wide, beautiful, playful, and mysterious, all in one. They were so animated she could simply communicate all of her thoughts without once moving her lips. Those were the eyes that had made her a movie star, and those were the eyes that had peeked into his soul and taken a piece of who he was with them. Yes, it was that look she gave him that scared him the most; it was a look that made him want to love her even when he knew the improbability of her loving him back.

After carefully drying each other, they returned to his bedroom and, still naked, lay down and snuggled in the bed, cloaked only in a blanket of darkness.

"Are you still awake?" Eris asked twenty minutes later.

"I couldn't sleep if I tried."

"Me neither," she said. Still facing the wall, she asked, "What was it like where you grew up?"

Troy thought it a strange question to ask someone you were lying in bed naked with, but he didn't mind. He would have answered any question that she asked, simply because he enjoyed the beauty of her soft, raspiness voice. It was a bedroom voice, one that he had the unique pleasure of experiencing directly.

"I grew up in Gloucester, not too far from Williamsburg and Yorktown. It's in the eastern part of the state, just off the water. I'd have to say that it was nice. A lot of history in the area. Also, there's a lot of natural beauty with the beaches and trees and trails. My mother is a librarian, so I spent a lot of time there, reading books and stuff. My dad is an optometrist with an office in Newport News. Neither one of them is from the area, but they had moved there a year before I was born and had decided to stay, so that's where I ended up growing up. What about you? What was it like in Louisiana?"

"I enjoyed Monroe. Relatively speaking, we have a pretty good parish, and we don't have some of the problems of larger cities like Shreveport and New Orleans. On the other hand, we don't have the same kind of entertainment, either. Shreveport and New Orleans have the casinos, the tourists, the sporting events, and the money. Monroe is just a plucky place where people handle their business and try to do the best they can. I think it's a great place to grow up, but for what I wanted to do with my life, Monroe couldn't do it for me," Eris said.

"Maybe one day you could show me around there," Troy said.

Eris let the comment fall flat and waited a beat before speaking again. "I have a question for you. What is it that you see happening between us?"

"I don't know. I would definitely like to date you with an eye towards something serious and exclusive. I'm really into you, and I'm open to all of the possibilities."

Eris laid her head upon Troy's chest. "I need to ask you something."

"Shoot."

"My age is not going to be a problem for you, is it? I mean, I know you said you were cool, but once the novelty of the newness of things wears off, will you still feel the same way?"

"I guarantee that it won't be an issue. You don't get it. You're my dream girl. I have fantasized about you for quite a while, and being here with you like this is beyond anything I could have ever imagined," he said.

Eris didn't respond, only nuzzling her head against his chest.

They lay in silence while the sound of the occasional car passing through the night streets or the soft breeze tiptoeing off the East River found its way against the window sill. Pretty soon Troy could hear the deep breaths of Eris's sleep, and he closed his eyes, capping off one of the most amazing nights of his life.

9

DREAMS

Troy awoke the following morning from the sound of Eris moving around the bedroom.

"Good morning," he said, barely opening his eyes. "You wanna get some breakfast? There's a great diner about a block away. Pancakes like you wouldn't believe!"

"No, that's all right," Eris responded, sitting in a chair across the room, facing the bed. She was putting on her stiletto heels and had already dressed in her clothes from the previous night.

"Are you leaving?"

"I need to get home."

"Are you coming back? I was kinda hoping maybe we could spend the day together or something like that."

Eris finished putting on her shoes and looked up. Her eyes met Troy's and she held that gaze for a moment before shaking her head. "I'm not coming back."

"Plans for the day already? Well, what about tomorrow?"

"Troy, I'm not coming back to see you at all while you're here."

Troy jumped up from the bed and walked over to her, taking her hands in his. "Why? Did I do something wrong? I thought we had a good time last night."

"It *was* nice, but I can't do this."

"Do what?"

"*This*," she said, waiving a hand around the room. "The truth is that I shouldn't have stayed over last night. And I probably shouldn't have done any of the things I did with you before. That was careless of me. I had my guard down."

Troy took a seat on the ottoman near the chair. "I'm so confused right now. Where is all of this coming from? Do you have someone special in your life already?"

"It's not even about that. I'd rather we just cut our losses here."

Troy reached for his clothes and started dressing while Eris grabbed her tote bag. He followed her out of the bedroom and into the den.

"Just tell me what I did wrong, so I can fix it," he said, following her across the room.

She stopped and turned to face him. "You said something last night that made me realize that this wouldn't work no matter what we did."

Troy reached for her hand and guided her to the sofa. "Let's sit down and talk. Even if you decide to leave, we can at least know that we understand what the other is thinking. Can we at least do that?"

She nodded and took a seat next to him.

"Okay. What did I say that rubbed you the wrong way?"

Eris looked away, either embarrassed or distraught by what she was going to say. Troy could not tell how to interpret any of her actions at this point. "You called me your dream girl."

Troy was incredulous. How in the world was that a bad thing? Most women would have been flattered to high heaven and back if a man said those words to them. In that moment, he realized that he just didn't understand Eris, who was proving to be atypical of everything he had ever experienced with a woman during his lifetime. He took a deep breath and said as calmly as he could muster, "Eris, could you please tell me how what I said was a bad thing?"

"It's not just that time, but you've said things throughout the entire time we've been hanging out that make me feel like you're not really interested in *me*, but in who you think I am. You have me on this pedestal in your mind, like I'm some kind of queen. If I weren't famous, I doubt you'd even be interested. I definitely wouldn't be your *dream girl.*"

Was she serious? Troy felt blindsided by what he figured was a mountain of insecurity on her part. "I didn't mean that you were my dream girl because I knew who you were before we met. I'm so past the fact that you're famous."

"Are you really?"

"Yes."

"Then why don't I believe you?"

Troy sighed. "I can't tell you what to believe or not believe. All I can tell you is that I have been 100 percent genuine with you from the first moment we met. And wasn't it you who told me to not assume I knew what you were thinking earlier? At least give me some credit that you don't really know what I'm thinking either. You don't know if I'd be interested in you or not. I get that. But if I tell you that I'm interested in you and that my reasons for being interested in you are because of the way you make me feel, I don't think you should ignore that just because you're worried about experiencing something new."

Eris grabbed her bag and stood. "I have to be able to trust your intentions, and right now, whether they are true or not, I can't tell. And since I can't tell, I have no choice but to protect myself."

"Protect yourself from me? Eris, I would never, I mean *never*, do anything to hurt you. But I'm starting to think that it doesn't matter what I tell you anymore. Just look at my actions. I have not taken advantage of your trust. I have not even told anyone about our spending time together. But you already know all of this. So what's really the deal?"

"It's just hard for me," she finally admitted through an exasperated sigh. It was as if she blamed herself just as much as she did her partner. "The last time I dated someone who wasn't in the industry, he tried to take pictures of me and sell them to a tabloid. The entire situation was embarrassing and hurtful. I felt like such a fool for thinking he and I had something special."

Troy placed a hand on Eris's shoulder. "I'm not him. That's all I can say. I would never do that to you. That's not who I am."

"I'm not trying to take this all out on you, but I need some space right now. I've already called for a car, and it should be here in a minute."

He shrugged his shoulders. "At least let me sit with you while you wait."

"Okay," she said softly.

They both sat back on the sofa, and Eris turned her attention to the rest of the room, looking at the art and photography on the walls, avoiding eye contact with Troy.

He sat back on the sofa with his head lifted to the ceiling, trying to not let the situation frustrate him while she sat so closely.

"The first time I heard 'Big Poppa' was at a step show the year before I pledged. I was like 'Who is this dude?' His voice was heavy and lispy. I remember a journalist saying that it sounded like a 'wet explosion.' But in spite of that, his flow was original and smart, you know? It was refreshing how smoothly he told stories."

Eris turned her attention back towards him, so he continued, "Back when Tupac died, I didn't believe it for two seconds. He had been shot before and survived. I figured he couldn't be killed—at least not with bullets. He died on Friday the 13th, too. It was one of those evenings that felt strange. I couldn't stop thinking about him for weeks. Then in March, Biggie. It all felt so strange. How did two of the best emcees in the game wind up dead? Hip-hop used to be fun. I remember doing the prep to L.L. Cool J's 'Around the Way Girl' and now I was seeing my favorite emcees get buried.

"I don't even know why I'm telling you any of this. I just know when Aunt Flo asked me if I wanted to housesit for her, I didn't hesitate to accept her offer. After all, this is Brooklyn. Maybe not Brooklyn like Bed Stuy, but it's still the borough. It just felt like the place I was supposed to be. And then you came along, and it was beautiful.

"And now you're leaving, and I guess it shouldn't matter, since I'll be heading back to Gloucester before the end of the month, but it does. It cuts me deep that you think you can't take me at my word. And I realize there's nothing I can do to convince you otherwise at this point. If this winds up being the last time we talk, I just want you to know that you have given me one of the most wonderful times of my life. The whole situation is the illest, though. I always found certain words to be funny because they mean opposites, like sanction and sanction, and the word 'ill' is like that. It's good and bad, and when I used that word with you earlier, it was all good. Now, it feels like it could go either way, because I'm happy for the time we're spending, but I'm sad that you feel you can't trust me about my feelings for you."

Just then Eris's cell phone rang, and she quickly answered. Once she hung up, she said, "The car is downstairs. I have to go."

Troy nodded. "So you don't have any response to anything that I've said?"

"What do you want me to say?"

"Say that you'll give me a chance."

Eris walked down the stairs and Troy followed her. As she reached for the front door, Troy grabbed her hand and stopped her, pulling her body to his, and kissing her deeply. She allowed him to enter her mouth, and she quickly reciprocated. Then almost as quickly as it had begun, it ended.

"You were always a good kisser," she said, opening the door and walking across the sidewalk to the car. Troy stood in the doorway watching her.

He waived to her as the car pulled away from the curb, but due to the tint on the windows, he couldn't see if she returned his wave or not.

He wanted to believe that she had seen him, but he was no more convinced of that than she had claimed to be of his feelings toward her.

She would figure out he was telling the truth, he knew. He just hoped that she did so before he was gone.

10

DENOUEMENT

In the days that followed, Troy found himself staying close to home, in hopes that Eris would call or perhaps stop by the brownstone. But with each day silent, no different from the last, it dawned on him that maybe this *was* the end. Maybe the arc of their story had climaxed around the same time their bodies had. The slow days leading toward Aunt Flo's return were the denouement, unsatisfactory as it was.

He used her phone number once during the second day after her departure and left a message, where he reiterated some of the same points that he had the last time she was there. He never received a call back.

He had also spent a few hours out of each day wandering the promenade, hoping to cross paths with her.

Their ending had come too abruptly, and he was ill-prepared to spend his last days in Brooklyn alone and was astonished that he'd allowed himself to be there for nearly a month and only make one friend the entire time. He knew that he was not the most sociable of people, but this was totally unlike him to not meet *anyone* outside of Eris Perry.

His loneliness gave way to fatigue, and during the day before Aunt Flo was to return (and he was to leave), he packed up all of his things, choosing to spend the final twenty-four hours of his Brooklyn Heights adventure living directly from his suitcase.

For lunch, he walked across the way to Fulton Street, where the cacophonic blend of music and street activity was the antithesis of the quiet, peaceful streets of Brooklyn Heights. The shopping area reminded him of 125th Street in Harlem. Posters and t-shirts of Biggie hung in windows, vendors spread out bootleg movies on blankets in front of stores, and every manner of oil-based fragrance, handmade jewelry, and artwork could be found along the sidewalks. He had only been to this neighborhood a few times, but he knew he wanted to at least come back one more time—maybe just to say goodbye. He grabbed a sandwich from one of the bodegas lining Fulton, bought a t-shirt of Biggie standing on a corner in Bed Stuy throwing dice, and headed back toward Brooklyn Heights.

He had already given up checking for Eris in the ocean of black people filling the neighborhood. Instead, he observed every conceivable shade of brown, a tableau of the uniqueness of a people, moving about. If Eris were out there somewhere, Troy chose not to separate her from the milieu of Afrocentricity that lay before him.

By the time he made it onto Montague, he had already

begun to visualize what was coming in the next few weeks. He would only be home in Gloucester for a few weeks before he flew out to California to begin the next phase of his life.

The idea of being a student filmmaker in Los Angeles was intimidating on a number of levels. All of the major movie studios were within half an hour of the school, and he had heard that it was not uncommon for directors and producers to drop by the schools (some of them their alma maters) to see what was new—or better yet, who was the new talented kid on the block. And with it being 1997, the word on the street was that black directors were on the rise. The industry had clearly come a long way from the days of Oscar Micheaux.

When Troy had first taken an interest in film, it had been because of Spike Lee's *School Daze*. It had started there, but he would eventually go back and watch all of the films made by Melvin Van Peebles and Gordon Parks, too. There was even a kid named Matty Rich who had made some noise in New York with *Straight Out of Brooklyn*. John Singleton, however, was the reigning black director on the block when Troy made it to Ellison-Wright. *Boyz in the Hood* had been a classic that, for better or worse, inspired a number of other films with darker urban themes, like the Hughes brothers' ultra-violent gangster movie, *Menace II Society*.

Troy had not yet decided what types of films he wanted to make, only that he wanted to make them. Having grown up on a steady diet of Stephen King and Edgar Allan Poe, he was leaning towards more macabre content, but he was open for the moment. He couldn't point his finger to any famous black directors who had done horror movies, other than Rusty Cundieff with his movie *Tales From the Hood*, a film that bordered on being comedy just as much as it was billed as horror. The absence of any other known black directors in the genre was more of an invitation than a turn off, as far as Troy was concerned. He would just need to make the film that would open doors for other young black directors.

His mind was still racing with thoughts of his film-making future when he arrived at the brownstone. He half-expected to see another note attached to the front door, one where Eris apologized for what happened and offered to make amends during his last evening. That idea didn't make much sense, though. She had gone more than a week and a half without contacting him, and he was unclear of when she was leaving for Vancouver to shoot her new film. It was like he was never a part of her world. The three times he had been with her seemed like moments where their worlds had just happened to collide—with a fury—and afterwards it was like the moments never even happened.

Troy hated the idea that he could share an intimate moment with a woman he truly liked only to have her disappear into thin air the next day. If this were a movie, he figured, there would have been some kind of happy ending. For example, there would have been a note on the door, or as he walked into the brownstone, there would have been something there waiting for him, an apology of sorts—or even a chance for him to apologize (for what, he was unsure). Or maybe there would have been a voicemail for him (of course there wasn't). Yeah, if this was a movie, he figured, that audience would have walked out of the movie pissed off that real life had trumped the fantasy of predictability.

He walked upstairs to his bedroom and marveled at how clean the space was. When he had arrived, it looked like an unused guest room. He had quickly transformed it into a lived-in room, one that bore more of his particular style. Now the room had gone full circle, and it looked as it had when he first arrived. He had already washed all of the dishes and cleaned up the sections of the room that he had frequented. He wanted Aunt Flo to return to an immaculate place, and once he removed his suitcase and backpack, it would be as if he had never been there.

He would miss the brownstone, true, but he was also ready to leave. He missed Gloucester and his parents, and the friends he had grown up with. He needed that time to be loved and doted on before he left for his new home on the West Coast.

He was so absorbed in his thoughts, that he almost missed the ringing of the phone. He picked up the cordless on the dresser in his room.

"Hello?"

"Hello, is this Troy?"

"Yes."

"This is Regina, Eris's assistant. I've been trying to call you for a few days now, but I accidentally mixed up the last two numbers in your phone number. I just realized it this afternoon, and I wanted to reach out to you and pass along a message from Eris."

Troy thought to himself, "Not this shit again." Regina had to have been the most incompetent personal assistant in the entire industry who still had a job. Getting the delayed message was akin to standing outside in the heat, sweating through his dress shirt, waiting outside a club where the bouncer took pleasure in his discomfort.

"Hi, Regina. What's the message?" His voice was flat and pained. He felt like he was on the verge of getting on the merry-go-round again: Eris charms him and makes him feel incredible; she then abandons him and then comes back to pick him up off the ground, but she has trouble contacting him before finally finding him; and the cycle repeats.

"She wanted me to tell you that she's on location in Vancouver right now but she will be in L.A. in October. I believe she said you'd be at USC this fall. Anyway, she wanted to see if you'd be interested in getting together for dinner."

Troy laughed.

"I'm sorry," Regina said. "Did I say something funny?"

"No, I'm just trippin' that she can book a dinner months in advance."

"That's just Hollywood," Regina said. "You plan out as far as you can."

"I see."

"She has an opening on October 17th at six o'clock. Should I pencil you in?"

Pencil me in, Troy thought. So this was how it was going to be with Eris? That did not sit well with him. He wasn't Eddie Murphy, she wasn't Robin Givens, and this wasn't *Boomerang*.

Still, he couldn't deny there was still a big part of him that longed to see her, if only for a moment. Maybe he could build with her that trust she so desperately needed with him to move forward. Clearly, she wanted the same thing as he, or she wouldn't have bothered reaching out to him.

He thought about lying in bed, back-to-back with her, hearing her moans creeping up his back into a thunderous, orgasmic punctuation. He thought about standing beneath the hot spray of the shower, washing her, his hands caressing her naked skin. He also thought about the feeling of her head lying on his chest, her soft breaths tickling him. There was definitely something there. She didn't have to take him to dinner or take him to the fashion show or even spend the night with him, but she had done all of those things. She was just trying to get herself into a space to feel better about what they were doing.

Maybe that was it.

Or maybe this was a game to her. She knew she could treat him any type of way and get away with it, because he was totally into her. She knew how to turn on her charm and how to manipulate him, if she needed to. There was not a single thing that had happened since Troy met her that was not in some way controlled by Eris. In many ways, he felt like an enthusiastic puppet.

He was torn, his ambivalence clouding his thoughts, as his fingers adjusted themselves around the phone.

Was there a future with Eris Perry, or did only confusion and heartache lie ahead?

Troy glanced around his bedroom, seeking traces of Eris within the space.

She had been there, right?

It was now difficult to tell. He closed his eyes trying to remember the taste of her kisses, the kisses that she claimed to have liked as much as he.

"Troy, are you still there?" he could hear Regina say. Her voice was not brazenly abrasive, but beneath its smooth, somewhat smug, timbre was the scraping quality that served as a reminder of this ever so slight hierarchical stratifier. Her boss was famous; he, however, was not.

"Yeah, sorry about that. The phone connection was a little weak where I was standing."

"Oh, okay. Well, is the 17th of October good for you?"

So this was what it all boiled down to, he thought, as he slowly paced back and forth across the hard wood floor of the room. This was the solitary thing that stood between him and Eris.

Seemingly simple. A one-word answer, at best.

He held the receiver close to his mouth, his lips parting, aching desperately not to betray his sense of self. He deserved a respect Eris had not entirely shown him, and he thought briefly about holding out, forcing her to be more respectful of his time and feelings, to stop playing games, and to even give him the benefit of the doubt that he would not be the asshole that her last boyfriend was. Surely he could demand at least these few things of her before he committed any more of himself to this situation, but who was he kidding? This was Eris Perry.

Maybe she had been right when she said that he would be unable to see her as anything other than famous—well, maybe not in those exact words—and he had wanted to reject that idea a hundred times over, but with Eris's assistant on the phone scheduling a date months in advance, he could not help but be reminded of this basic, incontrovertible fact.

He knew before he heard the sound of his voice, nearly bass-less from mild disuse and almost a muddled tinny whisper, that his response to Regina's question would be simple, plain, and unadulterated: "Yes."

Dancing in My Dreams

Originally published in
Spaces Between Us: Poetry, Prose and Art on HIV/AIDS,
edited by Kelly Norman Ellis

The city was just as I had remembered it in my dreams.

The taxi drifted serenely up the West Side Highway, sailing past the silhouetted skyline that had once been our playground. As I caught a view of the Hudson River glimmering from the reflections of a million lights rippling across its surface, I could see Serena's face. I could feel its warmth against my fingers as I pulled her into our last kiss that November day three years ago. Her perfume still tickled my nostrils like a phantom haunting me in the most delicious sense of the word.

There was no acceptable explanation for why I had left.

Sure there was the opportunity to study on the West Coast, but love should have made me unpack my bags. Her tears alone should have forced me to defer for at least another year—just until she could get her own situation worked out. But my own dreams called out in voices so strong that I could hear nothing else.

She had begged me not to go; I had asked her to come. When she refused to accept my invitation, I took it personally, and from there our relationship disintegrated, and our love, once a ripe fruit bubbling with the sweetest nectar I had ever tasted, withered slowly on the vine from neglect.

Why I had chosen to pack a bag and fly across the country late in the evening to see her wasn't even all that apparent to me. All I knew was that I had to let her know that I didn't want to move forward in this life without her by my side.

I had no specific idea of what I would do next if she were to commit herself once again to our love, but I was prepared to stay in New York until we were able to figure that out.

The e-mails had been short and sweet, reminiscent of the way things were when we were together. She said that she missed me, that she still loved me. I told her that I had made the ultimate mistake when I left her. Even her melodic voice over the phone soothed the ache of regret I had come to know in the solitude of her absence.

"We can try again," I stated emphatically in our last conversation.

"But you're there. And I'm here," was her response.

I didn't know if that was an excuse or an invitation.

And now in the depth of the evening I was seated in the back of a taxicab headed to Harlem, a solitary duffle bag resting beside me and a heart full to capacity of a love that refused to die amidst the trials of three years.

I imagined her as she appeared in the pictures she e-mailed me: her hair short and naturally curly, her eyes wide with tenderness, her smile framed by dimples, her teeth glistening pearls, her skin a flawless sheet of silk dipped in caramel and draped around an exquisite and well-formed frame. How could I have ever walked away from her?

The taxi eased into her neighborhood, a neighborhood in which I had spent many nights intoxicated from our lovemaking only to stumble back onto the train in the morning and barely make it to work on time. With the reflection of the street lamps against the brownstone, I felt as if I were gazing upon a castle, and inside that castle was the woman fate had revealed to be my queen.

Moments after I pushed the buzzer, the intercom rang to life with her sleepy voice.

"Serena, it's me. Kyle," I said.

"Kyle? Oh my god!"

Over the intercom I could hear her shuffling things around and then the door buzzed and unlocked, allowing me entrance.

The building hadn't changed much, but my mind registered every picture on the walls as something brand new. Reaching for the handrail, I ascended the stairs slowly, unsure of what her reaction to my presence would be.

I was prepared for anything. If there was someone in there with her, I would just deal with the situation as best I could. I had come prepared to win this woman's heart, and if it meant I had to confront someone else to get my point across, that was just the cost of following my heart.

She was already standing in the doorway looking very surprised when I reached the top of the stairs. Dressed only in a white ribbed tank top and a pair of tight jeans, she embraced me excitedly. For a moment all I could do was hold her, squeeze her, as if I was trying to absorb three years of lost warmth from her. She snuggled into my embrace and held on as if she shared my sentiment.

"I missed you so much," I said. "I had to see you."

"I missed you, too," she responded.

After what seemed like one beautiful, interminable moment, she released my body and took me by the hand, guiding me into her dimly lit apartment, the only lighting coming from night lights placed strategically throughout her apartment and a solitary lamp resting on a coffee table in her living room.

"What are you doing *here*?" she asked, still registering my presence in New York.

"After our last conversation, I had to come here to let you know that I am real about how I feel."

"And you couldn't have told me over the phone?"

My eyebrow lifted involuntarily as if I had just been swatted across the face with a thin white glove. I replayed her question in my mind, searching desperately for some semblance of humor beyond the words, only to find that the words lay bare.

"Did I miss something?" I asked.

She stood up, and without answering my question, offered me a drink. I accepted a Smirnoff Ice, but a sip from the cool beverage did little in the way of easing my nervousness.

"It's really nice seeing you though," she said.

"Are you sure? I mean, I'm starting to think that maybe you didn't want me to show up here like this."

"It's just a surprise, that's all."

"And obviously not a good one."

She looked at me carefully and took a swallow of her drink. "It's a good one."

"So what's wrong then?" I asked.

"Nothing's wrong. Well, not really wrong. It's just that your being here is giving me all kinds of mixed emotions," she responded.

"What do you mean?"

In the silence that followed my question, I could have died a million times. I tried to fix my gaze on her and will her to speak, but her patience wore me down. What little control I had over the conversation evaporated in the time it took her to open her mouth and speak again. This was clearly her show, and I was along for the ride.

"A lot's changed since the last time we were together," she said slowly.

"Are you seeing someone new or something?" I asked, fully aware that this was the greatest of the probabilities.

She lowered her head, losing herself in the slight swaying of the Smirnoff bottle in her right hand. "No. I'm not involved with anyone—any more."

A strange feeling came over me as I digested the weight of her words. Clearly there was someone after me, but it seemed as though that experience had taken a toll on her. I wanted to ask about what had happened while I was away, but I knew that it was better to leave our pasts behind us if we were going to move forward.

I reached over across the space between us on the sofa and rested my hand on her leg. She placed her hand over mine, and I half-expected her to remove it, but she didn't.

I carefully crafted my next words and began, "Hearing your voice again after all of this time has been one of the most beautiful and unexpected things to happen to me in quite some time."

At this comment, she smiled and rubbed her hand across mine. My skin tingled from her touch, itching and aching to be rubbed by her delicate, yet strong fingers.

I continued, "I just wanted to know if we could be together again. Serena, I love you."

She lowered her head and turned away from me. Raising a hand, she brushed it across her eyes, leaving the traces of tears along her face and hand.

In her silence, I felt prompted to ask how she felt. "Do you love *me*?"

She turned to face me, and looking deeply into my eyes, she nodded her head. "Yes. I love you."

"Then what's wrong? Did I upset you?"

"No."

The word was so soft that I found myself leaning in to catch the syllable as it brushed across her lip. My lips touched hers, and we kissed each other briefly. As she stopped and leaned back, I edged forward, kissing her again. This time my tongue found its way through the space between her lips, and I felt her tongue meet mine.

No sooner than the kiss began, it ended with her pushing her hands into my chest, moving me back to my side of the sofa.

"What's wrong?" I asked again, starting to become irritated by her lack of forthrightness.

"A lot's changed since the last time."

"Like what?"

Her next words fell into the vacuum of silence in such a way that they were suspended in mid-air. "I'm HIV positive."

For a moment I didn't even register her comment in my brain. I just stared at her in utter shock. Slowly the nature of the situation dawned over me as I found myself mumbling those three letters. Then I felt my own stomach plummet as I realized that she had to have contracted it from somewhere. Was it me? Was I HIV positive and didn't know it?

Reading my mind, she spoke again, breaking the silence that followed her initial comment. "I got it a little over a year after you left. I had been dating this guy named Torrance, and he found out that he had gotten it from an earlier relationship and didn't know it and that I should get tested. Shortly after I found out that I was positive, he moved back to his hometown in Ohio. He wanted to be at home if he became sick."

She took another long sip from her Smirnoff Ice and continued. "I got so depressed I almost took a bottle of sleeping pills. I just wanted out. I *really* wanted out. But as I sat there writing my letter and getting ready to take my pills, I just realized that I wasn't ready to die. Not like that. There were still things I wanted to do in life.

"When you got back in contact with me, I had gotten used to living each day to the fullest. That's why I opened up to you so quickly. That's why I told you how I felt about you. I have never loved anyone the way that I love you, and I know that I will always love you, regardless of what happens to us."

"Man," I sighed. I didn't know what to think. My mind was in a deep haze, and as I sat on the sofa, it felt as though my body was completely numb.

"I was going to tell you soon. We were just starting to get re-acquainted, and we hadn't gotten to the point where I felt comfortable telling you that. I had no idea that you would pop up here on my doorstep. I would've never wanted you to find out this way."

I opened my mouth to speak, and I was surprised when my voice choked in my throat and my eyes became glassy. I realized that I didn't really know what to say, so I reached out my arms to her and took her warmly into my embrace. I held on to her as if letting go would cause my body to collapse.

"It's OK," she whispered repeatedly in my ear. "I'm going to be OK."

When I finally released her, my face felt like it had been lifted to the sky during an April shower. Tears collected along my jaw line, and she brushed them away with her hand. In my feeling of hopelessness, I failed to recognize the immediate irony of her gesture: I was the one who was crying this time, not her.

"I love you," I told her.

"I know," she responded.

We sat in silence for a moment. I had not decided how long I would stay in New York when I arrived, and I didn't know what to do at this point. We could go on being friends until we could be friends no more, and I could return to the safe confines of my own Californian existence, or I could stay in New York indefinitely as I planned my next move.

"You're welcome to stay the night," she said.

"Whoa! Are you kicking me out tomorrow?"

I had already concluded that I would be staying the night with her, so when she couched the statement in those exact words, I knew that there was something more to it.

"I'm not kicking you out. You know I wouldn't do that. But I think you should get on back to California. I know that this is a lot to digest and that you probably need some time to yourself to take this all in." She placed the empty Smirnoff bottle on the coffee table in front of the sofa.

Although she had a point, I wrestled with her on leaving so soon. She told me that she had an audition for a play the next day and that she would be singing at a wedding the day after. In other words, there was no need for me to stick around.

"What about us?" I asked. The question had been looming beyond the horizon the entire evening, and now it was out there, a living, breathing thing.

"Can't we just be happy in knowing that we love each other without needing to re-build a relationship around it?"

"But I want you."

"Kyle, don't you see? I'm HIV positive. This can't work. It just can't!"

I dropped my head. "But I love you."

She stood up slowly from the sofa and looked me in my eyes. "You're a sweet man," she said, as she walked back to her bedroom and closed the door.

Alone in the room, I reclined on the sofa and gazed up at the ceiling. The whole evening had been surreal. I could not believe that I had jumped on a plane so quickly to come to New York. I also could not believe that everything she told me was real, although I knew deep down that she had no reason to be dishonest with me.

I closed my eyes, locked in thought, and found myself reflecting. I relived the moment that I saw Serena, as she stood singing on the stage of that Brooklyn poetry club. I remembered that first conversation, that first date, that first kiss. I relived dancing with her against the skyline of the city as her band members played beautifully in the background. I relived leaving her, and I relived that pain and anguish of not having her in my life any more. But here she was telling me that she was sick, and that she was not willing to chance another relationship with me. A dull ache spread throughout my body.

I rose from the sofa and went to her bedroom door, knocking gently.

"Come in," she said so softly I could barely make out the words.

I walked into the dark bedroom, removed my shoes, and lay down on the queen-sized bed next to her. My arm moved around her waist, and she laid her arm over mine.

We didn't speak, but I held her tightly until we both fell asleep.

The next morning, Serena arose early and began to prepare to leave for her audition. I decided I would leave the apartment when she left for her errands.

Standing in front of the brownstone that housed her apartment, I was at a loss for words. She placed her arms around my waist and leaned in to me, hugging me with all that her small frame could muster.

"I'm coming back," I said matter-of-factly.

She just looked at me.

"I want to be with you and be here for you."

"You don't have to do that," she said.

"I know, but I want to. You're the only one for me. And I don't know how all of this is going to work out, but I'm willing to try."

She looked up at me, and I held her face, kissing her gently on the lips.

"OK," she said softly.

"OK?"

"OK."

She released me, and I walked with her to hail a cab.

"Good luck on your audition," I said.

"Thank you. And you have a good flight."

I leaned over and kissed her again.

"I'll call you tonight when I make it back, and I'll start looking for another flight to come back in a few weeks. I have to tie up a few things before I come back."

A smile spread across her beautiful face. "OK."

A cab pulled up to the curb down the street from the brownstone, and I opened the back door for her. As she set one foot into the cab, she turned back to face me.

"Thank you for coming," she said.

"I'll be back soon. I promise."

"OK."

The cab pulled off slowly, and I walked down the block to hail another cab to get to the airport.

Shortly after my plane touched down in San Jose, I called Serena to let her know that I had arrived. After several rings, the voicemail came on prompting me to leave a message.

"Hi, baby," I said. "I just wanted to let you know that I made it back to San Jose. I'm about to catch a cab to the house. Give me a call when you get this message. I love you."

I hung up the phone, a smile spreading across my face. Although I tried to conceal them, my lips spread apart and my teeth came blazing through as if I were being asked to pose for a photograph on "Picture Day" in grade school.

When I returned to my apartment, I unpacked my duffle bag and put on Chaka Khan's "Through the Fire." As the melodies and lyrics wafted, I found myself completely lost within the song. As cliché as it might have sounded, the song allowed me to imagine us running towards each other across beautiful green meadows punctuated by the yellows, reds, blues, and purples of a thousand flowers.

I reclined on my bed, losing myself in the music as I stared at the ceiling. I hoped to be out of my apartment by the end of the month, and I could not wait to be next to Serena again. I wanted to hold her and let her know that we would fight this thing together, that I was prepared to be all that she needed me to be.

As the night began to draw to an end, I picked up my cell phone to check for any messages I might have missed due to a momentary signal loss, which I knew was always a distinct possibility given the location of my apartment. The signal was strong, and there were no messages, so I called Serena again. The phone went straight to voicemail, so I left another message.

Turning off the lights, I returned to my bed and lay down on my back, my cell phone resting on my chest set to vibrate when she called. I closed my eyes, and fatigue settled over me like a silk shroud. Within minutes, I drifted off to sleep.

I awoke around three in the morning and immediately checked my phone. The signal was still strong, and there were no messages. I didn't know why I had been so anxious to hear from her, but I felt as if seeing her had awakened something in me that had been dormant since I left New York. Patience was something that I no longer felt the urge to muster. My feelings were immediate, as was my need to express them.

After reluctantly returning to my slumber, I awoke around noon to a still apartment, sunlight trickling through my partially opened blinds. After checking my phone, I decided to walk over to the gym and work out for a while to free my mind from the prison of worry over Serena calling.

After an hour of pressing, pulling, and curling weights, my body stiffening with soreness, I returned to my apartment determined to not to focus on my phone not ringing. The day passed along quietly, and by the following morning, I decided to call her apartment again. When the voicemail came on, I immediately hung up the phone and dialed up the New York Police Department.

After being shuffled through the switchboard, I was finally connected to someone who was able to send a patrolman around to check Serena's apartment to make sure everything was all right. I left my number for someone to call in the event something turned up.

An hour later my phone rang. After having sat quiet for two days, the ring startled me. I ran into my bedroom to retrieve the phone from the bed, quickly scanning the caller ID. When I saw that the number was a New York number, I held my breath hoping to hear Serena's voice.

"Hello, may I speak to Kyle Taylor? This is Officer Madeline O'Keiffe with the New York Police Department."

"Oh, hi. This is Kyle."

"Mr. Taylor, I just wanted to let you know that we dispatched a unit already in the neighborhood to the address you requested. A Miss Serena Daniels answered the door and appeared to be in no distress. We notified her that we had been asked to look in on her and see if everything was all right. She told us that she was fine."

"Oh. Thank you. I appreciate your checking it out."

"No problem, Mr. Taylor."

As I hung up the phone, I sat down wearily on the edge of my full-size bed. I couldn't understand why Serena hadn't called me. Maybe I was just being paranoid; after all, she had informed me of her busy schedule before she left for the audition. At least I knew that she might still be in her apartment since the police had just left. Also, she had to have known that I was the one who sent the police to her apartment. I picked up my cell phone and dialed her number again.

The phone rang and rang until the voicemail picked up. Flustered, I left yet another message and hung up.

For the next few days, I resigned myself to the fact that I would never hear from her again. Her words seemed so empty as I replayed our last moments together. I felt forced to confront the issue of whether or not I had misread the signals.

It seemed clear that in the time between the moment she stepped in that cab and the moment I arrived in San Jose, something had changed. And whatever it was that had changed was haunting me with a silent vengefulness.

In the end, I never returned to New York.

I accepted a job offer with a small technology firm in the San Jose area after I finished my degree. It took me a while to get over Serena, and I felt as if I crashed much harder this time around. I don't know if it's because of love and the sensation of having found the person whom you believe is "the one." It could very well have been that I felt that I had an obligation to somehow rescue her from something that no one could or maybe rescue her from the pain I imagined that she was experiencing. Then it occurred to me that it could have been me who had needed rescuing, not her. Maybe it was one or all of those things, but maybe, just maybe, it was that eerie sensation of there being no closure that propelled me to fall so low this time. It seemed next to impossible that I could move forward in my social life without having an understanding of what went wrong.

The closest I came to a resolution was three months after what I would later recognize as my final visit to Serena's apartment. Tucked in with miscellaneous bills and my monthly issue of *Uptown* magazine was a postcard of The

Apollo Theater in Harlem. The postmark was from a New York City zip code; however, there was no return address. Only a simple phrase written in familiar penmanship danced across the page, lapsing into ellipses: *I couldn't....*

I tacked the postcard on the wall of my bedroom, and on the rare occasion these days when I become saddened by the hand life has dealt us, I attempt to fill in the ellipses of the card with my own dreams of us dancing together again —should we share another lifetime.

Simple Mathematics

Originally published in
Procyon Short Story Anthology 2014

"Come over here and talk to me," Elizabeth said, sounding more like Martin's grandmother than his wife of three years.

He shrugged his shoulders and relinquished his spot on the recliner. There was nothing on television anyway.

As he pulled up a dining room chair to the entrance of the kitchen, Martin admired how effortlessly his wife maneuvered around the rather large space, circling the island containing the stove and oven. As a foodie, he envied the grace with which she prepared dishes, but she was the chef, not he. He didn't know the first thing about proper knifing techniques or even how much attention was required to prepare the kinds of things Liz came up with. If it were not for her cooking proper meals for him, he'd still be overcooking anything that wasn't chicken.

"You're gonna love what I'm preparing for you tonight," she said, lifting a sauce pan from the gas stove and rotating its contents around with the fluid flick of her wrist.

"I can't wait."

Watching Liz, Martin realized he would much rather watch his wife's shapely figure, all 5'7" of her beautifully round body, move about their spacious kitchen than surf the myriad channels that came with their new satellite dish. He was often overwhelmed by the selections and found himself clinging to two or three channels, just to make sense of the cacophony of content.

Liz lowered the heat on the stove and turned towards Martin. "So there's this book that I've been reading by this relationship expert," she started.

He didn't know why, but suddenly his stomach began to bubble with anxiety. A relationship expert? He had thought that everything was perfect the way that it was. Why was she reading a book written by a relationship expert?

She continued, "And there were some things I wanted to run by you."

"OK," he offered, not wanting to shoot her down before hearing her point. They had had too many arguments in the past about his doing just that, so he was on guard to not stir the pot in the wrong direction.

"I have a very serious question to ask you."

His stomach tightened again, and he could feel the

slight rumble of gas rolling across his stomach cavity. "Go ahead."

She paused for a moment, and in that moment Martin knew that whatever she was going to say would more than likely lead to an argument if he didn't prepare himself to not say the first thing that came to mind. He had been working on the filter between his mind and his mouth, and that pause was exactly what he needed to do a gut check on that filter. *Prepare yourself for anything*, he told himself.

Rather than ask her question, Liz returned her attention to the stove, turning off the eyes. "Maybe we should eat dinner first. I'd hate for you to eat any of this cold."

"Is it that bad?"

"What? The food? Of course not!"

"No. I mean the question."

"It's not bad."

"But it's not good either," he said.

"It just is what it is. Whatever your answer is, everything will be OK."

With her words, Martin's appetite vanished. It was so sudden that he had no reaction to the Ahi steak, lightly sautéed spinach, and pilaf she placed on the dining room table. As he adjusted his seat to face the food, and then her, as she sat across from him, he realized how much better it might have been if his wife had not even brought up the topic prior to dinner.

"It looks delicious," he offered, "but I want to know what you're going to ask me first."

"It's not that serious. We can talk about it after dinner."

"Then why did you bring it up when you did, if it could have waited?"

At this, she was quiet. In that moment, Martin realized that she hadn't even considered the timing of her question. That meant that whatever she wanted to ask him was so important that it moved through her mouth faster than she wanted it to. Whatever it was, they would have to talk about it right then.

"Bon appetit!" she said, forcing a smile to her face.

"Liz, come on. Just ask the question. You're building this up into something big, so now I have to know."

He didn't know why he was paranoid about any of this. He had done nothing wrong—that he could think of. Still, deep down, he harbored a deep fear of divorce after witnessing what his parents went through when he was thirteen. His father had left his mother for another woman, and although he loved Liz with all his heart, he sometimes dreamt that she would come in one day and do to him what his father had done to his mother. As a result, he had pledged himself to making his marriage work at all costs, and although they argued regularly, he made sure that they didn't go to sleep angry at each other.

"OK," Liz said. "I'll ask, but I'd still like you to eat the food while it's hot."

Martin lifted his fork and eased it through the Ahi. The fish gave way beneath the weight of the utensil to reveal a brilliant purplish-red center. He took a bite, his eyes fixed on her.

"Have you ever thought about being with another woman?"

The question had been in the air at least three seconds before he realized what she was asking him. "No. Have you thought about being with anyone else?"

"Never?" she asked. Her eyes hinted at incredulity. "Not once?"

"You must have," he countered.

"I assumed it was just natural to think about things like that."

Martin put his fork down.

"So are telling me that you want to leave me?" Just saying the words aloud made him feel as if his heart was turning into crystal, fragile and capable of exploding into a thousand pieces in his chest.

"Calm down, Martin. I don't want to leave you. I love you. And I love this marriage. But I've been doing some thinking, and I think we should talk about this."

"What's there to talk about? You clearly want to have sex with someone else. Is it a woman? Lord have mercy, Liz. Don't tell me you're out there like that."

She sighed, measuring her breaths. "I'm not saying any of that. But if we're going to talk about this, we have to talk about it like adults. We are two grown sexual beings, and I need for you to get out of your own way long enough for us to have a serious conversation. Can you do that for me? Please?"

He had already prepared to come back with something to shut down this discussion, but the word "please" had softened him. Still beneath the surface, his mind remained a hardened steel. "Just tell me one thing. Where did you get this idea?"

"Like I said earlier, I was reading this book about how open marriages had certain long-term advantages over traditional marriages."

"So some sexual deviant with a PhD writes a book and now you think it's okay to jeopardize everything we have? I can't even believe that you'd fall for something like that," Martin said. He was nervous and exasperated and no longer wanted to talk about any of this.

"Dr. Blythe is not a sexual deviant. She puts forth a pretty compelling argument that aside from money and children, sex is the primary reason most marriages don't work. To keep an enthusiastic and healthy sex life is the purpose of her book. You should at least take a look at the book before you go and rule out everything."

Liz's interest in the book unnerved him, and he casually pushed his dinner to the side. "If you were unhappy with our sex life, you could have just told me. I mean, I know that I could try harder."

"It's not about trying harder. I love making love to you."

"Then why change it up with this nonsense?"

She inhaled deeply, her mannerisms deliberate, as if searching for another approach. "Before we got married, what was the freakiest thing that you ever did?"

Martin found himself considering her question reluctantly. He was afraid to admit to his wife that he had not done much beyond what might be considered standard sex.

He had never used any bondage devices, battery-powered toys, rings or clips. He had also never been a part of an orgy or anything else his college roommates had bragged about during his days at State. Liz had been the first woman on whom he had attempted cunnilingus, and it had taken him a while to perfect a technique that did not involve her having to constantly reposition his head and coach the movements of his tongue. If he had to rate himself as a lover, he knew that he was definitely a "B-" most of the time and a "B" on good days. Maybe if he didn't have the inhibitions he had about sex, he might have had an answer to give his wife to show that he wasn't as square as he believed himself to be.

"I once received a blowjob in the back of a cab," he lied. He didn't know why he said it, but if his marriage was about to go down the tubes, he figured it best to go out swinging.

"Did you like it?"

"It was nice."

"Would you like for me to give you a blowjob in the back of a cab?" Liz asked.

The idea had never crossed his mind. He had never imagined that they could be intimate outside of their bedroom. "You'd do that?"

"Sure. You're my husband. Why wouldn't I?"

Emboldened by her reply, Martin asked, "What is the freakiest thing that *you* have ever done?" He wasn't sure he wanted to know, but he felt that he had little choice in the matter now that he had already given an answer.

"I once had sex with a guy while my boyfriend watched."

She said it so matter-of-factly that Martin found himself flinching. Now it all made sense. She was reminiscing and decided that she still had a few fantasies to get out of her system. He tried to look at her, but at that moment all he could think was that his wife had been a slut. There was a part of him that felt that was an unfair assignation, but his pride stung from her honesty. Then he had another thought: she had settled for him when they married. Clearly, he wasn't even on a level to make her sexually happy, but she had gone through with it anyway. He could scarcely understand why she would do that, but even more, he was frightened by how this conversation would end. He wished he could rewind the clock and go back in time. At first, he thought about going back to before the conversation started, but then he realized it might be worth considering going back to a point before he proposed to her.

"Liz, I can't do this. Any of this. I'm just not built that way. I can't stand the idea of another guy inside of you. I can barely handle the idea of what your life was like before we met. Now I'm feeling strange knowing that you have all of these thoughts—urges—that I can't help you with. Maybe this conversation was a bad idea."

She reached across the table and took his hands in hers. "I would never make you do anything that you didn't want to do. You come first, and I would never consider doing anything that would undo the marriage that we have built. Please understand that." She paused, rubbing her thumbs over the backs of his hands. "When I thought about what you might say to my questions, a part of me thought that maybe you had thought about being with another woman. I asked myself how that made me feel. Yes, I was jealous. That's the natural reaction. Dr. Blythe said that overcoming jealousy was the key to removing the shackles of our fears. I closed my eyes and imagined you having sex with another woman. I was angry for a while until I saw the pleasure in your face. That's when I realized that I could get over my jealousy issues if it meant that it would make you happy."

Martin shook his head. She had actually spent time thinking about him being with another woman? Could he have done the same? He doubted it, but he could feel something rumbling deep down in his subconscious: curiosity.

"So if I wanted to have sex with another woman, you would be okay with that?" Although he had not given the idea any thought prior to that moment, he couldn't help scrolling through his mental database of women who had held their gazes at him a bit too long. If he were another man, he would have already exploited his options, but he was determined to make his marriage work and prove his parents' dissolution a non sequitur in his own life.

"Yes, I would. But would you be okay with me being with another man?"

Martin chewed on the inner wall of his cheek, his nerves abuzz with discomfort. "What if you got turned out?" He hated to even acknowledge the possibility, but he was a man. How could he not?

"I'm in love with *you*. You are my addiction. No man can change that," she answered.

"What if he's, you know, more *endowed*?"

"What if the woman you wanted to be with had larger breasts than mine?"

"Breasts and penises are two totally different things." His formality didn't escape Liz's attention.

"So what if I fucked a guy whose dick is bigger than yours? Your dick is perfect for me. Sex can't trump how I feel about you."

She had never referred to his penis as a "dick" before, and rather than be repulsed by her language, he was actually turned on—but was he turned on enough to consider any of the things she was proposing? He didn't think so.

"Will this keep you from leaving me?" he asked.

"I told you that I'd never leave you—regardless of what you decided."

Martin stared at his wife, his eyes sweeping slowly from her hair down to her sweet, angelic face, down to her neck and, eventually, her breasts. He imagined another man's hand cupped around one of them as he plunged himself into her, his other hand gripping her round ass firmly. His stomach bubbled, but he forced himself to not look away. Was it really as simple as getting over your jealousy issues?

"Can I see Dr. Blythe's book?"

"Sure. Hold on and I'll get it for you."

As she rose from the table, Martin called out to her, "I'm not saying that I want to go through with this. I just figured I'd at least take a look at the book."

"That's fine. I understand."

When Liz returned with the book, placing it next to his uneaten food, he took her hand. "Baby," he said, "how did we end up here?"

"Marriage is a journey," she responded. "A lot can happen between taking vows and staring off into the sunset as grandparents."

He wasn't sure if this was Liz's own wisdom or something she picked up from Dr. Blythe's book.

As he ran his fingers along the cover of the book, he looked longingly at Liz. Was it accurate to say that if he loved her, he would open it and read it? He didn't know. But looking into her eyes, he knew that he was going to do something that might have seemed a given with any other married couple, but was revolutionary as far as he was concerned: he was going to give his wife the benefit of the doubt.

B-Sides and Remixes

30 Love: A Novel

Mojo's Guitar: A Novel/ (Il était une fois Morris Jones)

Afro Nerd in Love: A Novella

The Keys of My Soul: A Novel

The Race of Races: A Novel

The Illest: A Novella

Bessie, Bop, or Bach: Collected Stories

Four Floors (with Sabin Prentis)

Black Hand Side: Stories

White Pages: A Novel

She Lives in My Lap

Reverb

Work-In-Progress

Daykeeper

Most of My Heroes Don't Appear On No Stamps

Portable Black Magic

Ran Walker is the winner of the 2019 National Indie Author of the Year Award (selected by judges from Library Journal, Publisher's Weekly, IngramSpark, St. Martin's Press, and Writer's Digest), the 2019 Black Caucus of the American Library Association Best Fiction Ebook Award, and the 2018 Virginia Indie Author Project Award for Adult Fiction. He is also the recipient of both a 2005 Mississippi Arts Commission/NEA artist grant and a 2006 artist mini-grant. He served as an Artist-in-Residence with the Mississippi Arts Commission in 2006. Additionally, he is a past participant in the Hurston-Wright Writers Week Workshop and is the recipient of a fellowship from the Callaloo Writers Workshop. He teaches creative writing at Hampton University and lives in Virginia with his wife and daughter.